Swept Away

~ Grayton Series ~
Willow & Caleb
© 2016 Jill Sanders

Follow Jill online at:
Jill@JillSanders.com
http://JillSanders.com
Jill on Twitter
Jill on Facebook
Sign up for Jill's Newsletter

Dedication

To my dad,
who helped open the door
to my imagination...

Summary

Willow has had a hard time trusting people, especially men, ever since her reckless father abandoned her at a young age for the romantic idea of life on the open road. After finally graduating from college, she's now enjoying her new job and carefree life on the beach. When an injured stranger shows up on her doorstep looking for her deceased dad, she is instantly thrust back into the dark past she's been trying to escape her whole life.

Cocky Caleb has never really had it easy, but lately, things have taken an extreme turn for the worse. Seriously injured and on the run from outlaw biker's hell-bent on controlling him, he seeks shelter with the only person who could possibly save him once and for all… if he can keep his smart-ass mouth shut.

Swept Away

by
Jill Sanders

Prologue

There wasn't much that nine-year-old Willow got really excited about, but seeing her father after he'd been gone for two months was one of them. Even if it meant her older sister, Wendy, was in one of her "moods."

Her big sister had forced her to help clean up their tiny apartment. Willow had even had to help clean the bathroom they shared, a job she had learned early on to avoid by pretending to puke every time she got near the toilet with the brush. This time, however, Wendy had made her clean even the mirror and the sinks all by herself.

After the great cleaning, the entire apartment smelled like pine and was even cleaner than when they had moved in almost a year ago. They both sat on the sofa in their Sunday dresses, waiting for the front door to swing open.

But, after what seemed like hours, Willow must have fallen asleep waiting, because she woke when Wendy picked her up and carried her into their shared bedroom. The room was so small, there was only space for the one bed, which Wendy always ended up giving to Willow. They had slept on the bed together until recently when her sister complained that she kicked in her sleep.

Willow had asked why Wendy didn't sleep in

their father's bed in the other bedroom, but her sister had never given her an answer.

As Wendy gently pulled off Willow's dress shoes and set them beside the bed, she asked, "When's daddy going to get here?"

Wendy tucked Willow's favorite silky blanket under her chin. "I'm not sure, sweetie." Her sister brushed a blonde strand of her hair behind her ear.

"I wanna stay awake." Willow pouted.

Wendy shook her head. "You have school tomorrow."

"But, Daddy—" she started.

"Willow, you know the rules." Her sister frowned down at her. Instantly, Willow shut her mouth. They had agreed to a set of rules the last time their father had left them alone. Willow had done her best to follow each and every one. Not that she was afraid of her sister. Wendy had been nothing but kind to her for as long as Willow could remember.

It wasn't fear that kept her from pouting now, but respect. Her sister had sacrificed so much for her, there was no way she was going to do anything to upset her. Not when she remembered the last time Wendy had gone out of her way to give Willow the new shoes she'd asked for.

After her Sunday dress was pulled from her, Willow rolled over and tucked herself into a tight ball. Silent tears streamed down her face at the thought that she wouldn't be able to see her father that night. When the dark thought crept into her mind that it might be months more before he'd come home, she curled herself even tighter and dreamed about the last time she'd seen either of her parents.

Several hours later, she felt a warm hand on her face and opened her eyes to her father standing over her.

"Daddy?" She reached up and rubbed her eyes to make sure she wasn't dreaming.

"Sweet Willa," her father whispered. Just hearing his nickname for her caused happiness to spread throughout her entire body. She launched herself out of the bed and straight into his waiting arms.

Her father smelled like booze and smoke, but she didn't care. Not once his arms wrapped around her and held her tight. She felt safe for the first time in months.

Finally, she pulled back and looked into his scruffy face. He looked a lot thinner than she remembered and there were dark circles under his eyes. She touched his long silver beard and, looking into his blue eyes, she asked, "Why did you stay away so long?" She whispered it since her sister was still asleep on her sleeping bag near the corner of the room.

"Places to see, people to meet." He chuckled and sat down on the edge of her bed, moving her onto his lap.

"How long are you staying?" She held her breath, fearing the answer.

"I'm back for good this time, Willa." Her father frowned as he glanced down at the floor. "Let's let your sister get some rest. I'll see you in the morning." He leaned down and placed a kiss on her forehead. "I've got a surprise for you."

Her father always bought her small gifts from the places he'd visited. The last time she'd gotten a small metal figurine of a dancing girl. She treasured every gift he'd given her and couldn't wait to see what he'd brought her this time.

She moved to sit up, but her father's big hands pushed her back down. She wanted to prolong her time with him.

"Tomorrow," he promised. "Go to sleep my sweet Willa. Sweet dreams."

She tucked her body back up into a ball and dreamed about spending the rest of her life with her daddy. But, fate was cruel, even to a nine-year-old. Less than six months later, Willow stood next to her sister as she spread their father's ashes into the ocean. The cancer had moved fast, turning the strong man she once looked up to into nothing more than skin and bones.

Willow vowed that day that her father would be the only man she would ever love.

Chapter One

Caleb Harris was in trouble. But what else was new. He glanced over his shoulder one more time and cursed under his breath. How could he have let his guard down? Then he remembered and cursed the sexy woman that had taken his mind off of his own dangers. Damn his soft spot for beautiful women.

Deciding it was now or never, he tucked the small package into his back pocket and took off at a sprint. He didn't know this part of town well, since he'd only arrived early last week, but he knew there was only one chance of getting away—being fast.

He'd been running his entire life. At least it seemed that way. That was, up until Billy had taken him under his wing.

The old man had been Caleb's savior back when he was living on the streets of Vegas. Caleb knew how to take care of himself; after all, he'd been on his own most of his life. His mother had been a showgirl by day and a call girl by night and never really had time to raise a kid. Nor had she had the skills.

The dirty little trailer she'd rented for the two of them had been nothing short of gross. He'd spent every waking breath trying to escape the hellhole. And most days he'd succeeded.

Since he'd been on the scrawny side as a kid, he'd spent most of his youth getting picked on and beat up by kids bigger than him. Until he'd joined his first gang at the age of nine. It had been nice to be part of a family for the first time in his life. Sure, he'd gotten into more fights than he could remember, but he'd felt like he was part of something bigger.

When Henry, the gang's leader, was picked up by the police and hauled away to juvie, the rest of the members had split. It had taken Caleb almost a whole year to find his next gang, which he'd stayed in until his first trip to juvie himself. During his time locked up, something wonderful had happened to him. He'd grown. Bigger and taller than most kids his own age. He quickly learned a valuable lesson about staying in shape and being able to run fast, which had taken him to a whole different level.

After he'd spent a few months in a boy's correctional home, his mother had pretty much told him that he was on his own. He didn't mind it much, especially after learning his mother had a new ass of a boyfriend living with her. He was better off by himself.

At the age of eleven, he couldn't have been more thrilled to be completely independent. And by the time he was thirteen, he'd grown so much that he could have easily been mistaken as a sixteen-year-old.

So, for the next few years, he'd done what he needed to in order to survive the streets, everything from selling drugs, running errands for other gang members, to being hired out as a carrier of sorts. The last job he'd had—delivering packages—had turned out to be the worst one and the luckiest at the same time. That's when he'd met Billy.

He'd stolen a car and delivered the package out to the gas station in the middle of the dessert. Upon arriving, he'd been jumped by two guys and dragged into a back room where he'd gotten the shit kicked out of him and told he was pretty much toast.

Of course, this only pissed him off and he'd stood up, wiped the blood from his face, and demanded double pay for the job.

He could still remember when a third guy walked into the room and laughed at him. Billy had stopped the other two guys from beating the shit out of him.

Billy had quickly taken Caleb under his wing and had protected him from the other guys. He'd taught him everything he needed to know to survive.

Less than a year later, he'd gotten Caleb his first bike and had stood by him when he'd been officially inaugurated him into the last gang he'd ever join.

Billy was the father Caleb had never had. The older man not only taught him what hard work was, but how to use his strengths to get what he wanted. Soon, Caleb was making his way up the ladder in the gang. Ralphie had been the leader of the Lone Outlaws for more than two decades, but Caleb and a few guys were talking about making some changes in the gang.

For the first time in Caleb's life, everything was going perfectly. Until the night Billy pulled him aside and told him his secret, and then proceeded to drop the biggest bomb ever… Billy was leaving the gang for good.

It had taken him less than two minutes to make up his mind to go with Billy. But everything Caleb had spent two years working for had gone up in smoke that night. He didn't even have time to pack or say goodbye. Instead, Caleb made a choice to start running, and he was still running thirteen years later.

Now, Caleb ran into a back alleyway and immediately regretted the move when he hit a dead end. Cursing, he turned around, only to be blocked by two shadows.

"Bout time we found you," Al sneered. The man's one eye gleamed in the dim light. The patch over his other eye was like a beacon, drawing Caleb's eyes to focus on its darkness.

"We've been lookin' long and hard for you, boy." Tony moved closer. Caleb knew not to let the skinny man fool him. Tony was a boxer and could take down the best and biggest. But spending the last thirteen years in jail hadn't been kind to either of the men. "Where you been hiding?"

Caleb was bigger and faster than the two older men put together, but it wasn't size or speed that had fear snaking down his spine. It was the two 9mms pointing directly at his chest.

"I've been laying low. You know, after all the mess. Besides, can't a guy just decide he needs a break?" Caleb tried to keep his voice calm as his eyes moved around the alley looking for any escape.

"Sure." Al smiled and nudged Tony. "You need a day or two here or there, but thirteen years?" He moved closer. "Thirteen fucking years!" he screamed, causing Caleb to flinch.

"It's time you came back home and paid for what you did," Tony added.

"I've paid. Besides, I'm trying this new thing." He'd backed up until he was pressed against a door. Thankfully, the knob turned easily in his hand. "It's called living," he said just as he pushed himself into

13

the doorway. He felt a stabbing pain in his side, but didn't stop as he raced through the back kitchen of a Chinese restaurant. He heard crashing behind him and guessed that Al and Tony were fighting with the kitchen staff, since he'd pushed a whole stack of dishes onto the floor as he'd raced by.

When he hit the front of the restaurant, he glanced around quickly and decided to race around the buildings and head back down the same alleyway. He hunched behind a large trash can as he tried to get his breathing in check.

The town was small enough that he knew it was almost impossible to lose the two men without outsmarting them. Besides, he didn't know who else from the gang was lurking in the shadows, looking for him. He hated that he'd parked his bike right in the middle of the main parking lot. He was pretty sure that Tony and Al were sitting there, watching it, waiting for him to return to his wheels.

He'd gotten the bike a few years ago, after he'd traded in the bike Billy had gotten him. This bike was bigger and more reliable. Plus, it had been his only means of escape. Which, he reminded himself, was now cut off.

He waited for what seemed like hours, listening, waiting, but everything remained silent. When it started to lightly rain, he moved a little and realized that both of his legs had gone to sleep. Cursing under his breath, he finally glanced down at his side and noticed the large pool of blood just underneath his hip.

"Damn." He felt his head spin. He'd been so concerned with listening for Al and Tony, he'd forgotten about the searing pain in his side. Actually, after the first few minutes of hiding, everything had gone numb.

He leaned back and tried to wiggle his toes. When he felt them move in his boots, he smiled. It took a few minutes for his legs to regain their feeling and in that time, he'd come up with a new plan.

Willow was tired and sore. She'd spent the last eleven hours out in the sun setting up barriers along the twenty-mile stretch of sugar-sand beaches.

Protecting sea turtles was the sole purpose of her life for the next few months. Not to mention her dream job.

She'd spent countless hours in school learning how to be a marine biologist. Who would have known that it would all come down to walking the beach and putting sticks in the ground?

She sighed as she let herself into her apartment. But she had to admit, she did love her job. When she wasn't cut loose on the beach, she was housed at the local marina working with and helping rehabilitate injured animals. But since it was her second year on the job, she'd been given the choice to head up the turtle conservation project. So far, her team had found and safely barricaded off over thirty-five hundred nests.

She'd been fooled into thinking it was an easy job at first, but after four weeks of nonstop working, she now knew better. She'd never added so many miles to her pedometer before and she'd lost almost ten pounds and two whole sizes. Not to mention that she was now nice and tan from all the time spent outdoors.

Shutting her apartment door behind her, she took a moment to look around her small space. It was all hers. No roommates, no big sister to clean up after her, no boyfriend to get in the way. She smiled a little when she remembered how much freer she'd felt after things had ended with her long time on-again-off-again boyfriend, Jake.

Shortly after she'd started going to Florida State University, Jake had surprised her by joining the army without asking or even telling her until the day before leaving for basics.

She'd tried to stay in touch with him, but a little over a year ago, she'd gotten word that he'd married and already had a kid.

She walked into the living room and dropped her large backpack on the floor, then fell backwards onto the secondhand sofa she'd bought for her space, sighing when she hit the soft cushions. Closing her eyes, she smiled.

This was the part of the day she liked the best, when everything was still and quiet. There was a light patter from overhead as the evening rain fell on her skylight.

Her dark locks were a little damp from the rain as she rested her head back on the sofa. She'd colored her hair a rich dark color only a few months ago. Normally, she'd spent hours and lots of money keeping her long locks a striking blonde, much like her sister Wendy still did. After graduation, when she'd moved closer to her sister near Surf Breeze and had taken the full time job at the West Florida Gulfarium, she'd decided that she needed a change. Besides, she thought the darker color suited her personality better.

Toeing off her shoes, she rested her feet on her glass coffee table and reached for the remote, just as a knock sounded at her door.

Occasionally, her sister liked to stop by before her evening shift bartending at the Boardwalk Bar and Grill. Pushing up from the sofa, she walked over and yanked open her door with a smile on her face. She was shocked at the tall, dark figure looming in her doorway. She moved quickly to slam the door shut and screamed when his hand reached in and held it open.

"Billy." His voice was rough as he used his weight to push the door open. "Where's Billy?"

Willow tried once more to shut the door, this time using all her weight, but he used his shoulder to hold it open and it didn't budge.

His dark eyes bore into hers and for a moment, she forgot to breathe. Dangerous. The word screamed in her head as she fought with him, trying to close him out.

Then she thought of trying a different tactic and moved away from the door quickly. The man's giant frame fell forward as the door swung open. She thought that he would catch himself before landing on her floor, but instead, he hit the tile in her entryway with a loud thud.

She was about to sprint past him and run to her neighbor's door for help, when she noticed the blood on his hands and clothes.

"Willa," he whispered as his dark eyes slid closed. "Billy."

Hearing her father's nickname come from his lips shocked her to her core.

"Billy?" She shook her head. "Billy Blake?"

The man on the ground groaned as he nodded. "Where is he?"

She stopped moving as her heart jumped in her chest. "He's dead," she blurted out.

The man made no move, so she trailed her eyes up and down him cautiously. She knew he was tall, since he had loomed over her in the doorway. He was wearing dark jeans with a black leather jacket and matching black boots. His hair was neatly cut, almost military style. From what she could see, he looked a few years older than her.

She jumped a little and watched as he rolled slightly to the side. Then she held in a scream when she noticed more blood gushing from his side, just above his hip.

Instantly, instincts took over. She was on her knees beside him, opening his jacket fully and ripping his T-shirt up the front. Her hands quickly covered the large gash on his hip, putting as much pressure as she could on it.

She didn't flinch this time when he cursed and rolled his head with pain.

"You need to go to an ER," she said as she felt his warm blood seep through her fingers.

"No!" He yanked her arms away from his hip. "No doctors or cops," he growled out between clenched teeth as he kicked her front door shut with his foot.

"Listen…" she started.

"Caleb," he broke in as his breathing hitched with pain.

"Listen, Caleb." Her eyes moved over him, searching for any other holes he might have in his skin. "If you don't want to see a doctor, that's up to you, but the way you're bleeding, it won't take long for you to lose every ounce you have." She pushed his hands away from hers and covered his wound once more.

Her eyes moved over to where she'd dumped her bag. She knew her phone was tucked just inside the side pocket.

He started to get up, but she shoved him back down, putting her hands on his shoulders. "Don't move," she demanded and then leaned over to grab her bag.

"No!" He wrapped his long fingers around her ankles and pulled her back towards him.

Instincts kicked in and she started to fight him. She kicked out, but somehow, he ended up pushing her under his hard body, holding her still with his weight. She tried to fight, but soon he was pinning her down and glaring at her.

"Promise me. No doctors and no cops," he demanded. His shirt was soaked with blood and water from the rain outside. Which meant that her shirt was now soaked as well, causing it stick to her skin.

His legs were holding hers down, no doubt to keep her from kicking him again. She felt his full weight holding her down and decided against struggling since she didn't want to injure him further.

"I can't help you." She moved slightly to push him off, but stopped when he moaned in pain. She felt his breathing hitch as he grabbed for his side. "You need a doctor," she said a little more urgently. She'd never met a more hardheaded man before, especially one that was obviously in so much pain.

"No," he said, still clenching his teeth. "No doctors."

"Stubborn." She glared up at him.

"Promise me." She could hear his voice waver and guessed that he was on the verge of passing out. But, looking into his dark eyes, she guessed that he'd hold onto consciousness until she made the promise.

Instead of finding her voice, she nodded her head as her eyes locked with his. He seemed to take a few moments to decide if she could be trusted before rolling off her. When his shoulders rested on her tile floor, his eyes slid closed.

"I'll need my things." She glanced over to her emergency bag after his eyes opened. She'd taken a Community Emergency Response Team class a few months back and had learned some basics about how to preform CPR as well as how to stop bleeding and stitch someone up. Everything she needed was in her neon green CERT bag which sat just behind her front door.

She pointed to it, and when he nodded, she moved over and pulled the heavy thing towards her.

He lay completely still as she doused his wound with alcohol. The fact that he didn't flinch as the cool liquid cleansed the deep gash told her so much about the man. He was used to pain. When his eyes opened and met hers, she could see even more pain behind the darkness there.

21

"I'll need to sew this up." She used a dish towel to wipe her hands clean.

He nodded once more.

She started to stand up, but he once more grabbed her ankle to stop her.

"Billy?" His voice was low and when she met his eyes once more, she knew what he was asking.

"Over twelve years ago to cancer." When he dropped his hand, she turned and walked into her bathroom.

Her hands shook as she pulled out her small sewing kit from under the sink. Setting it down on the counter, she rested her hands on the sink and leaned a little as she took a few deep breaths.

Who was he? How did he know her father? So many questions ran through her mind, but one question dominated. Who had hurt him and why didn't he want the police involved?

When she felt a little steadier, she walked back out to the living room. The man hadn't moved. As she leaned over him, his eyes slid open.

"You should swallow these." She held out two pills.

He shook his head and closed his eyes with a groan.

"Fine." She rolled her eyes and thought of calling him stubborn once more. "This is going to hurt."

He shrugged his shoulders and she watched him

22

tense as the sterile needle pierced his skin. She was so focused on her task that she didn't realize he had lost consciousness until after she had covered the wound with a large square bandage.

She sat over him for a few moments, debating what to do. Should she call the police, even though she had given him her word? She couldn't explain it, but she didn't feel as if she was in danger. Maybe it was because he was currently unconscious or maybe it was because she had seen something hidden behind those dark eyes of his.

Standing up, her eyes ran over him once more. His T-shirt was ripped open, showing off an impressive chest and the sexiest six-pack she'd ever seen. His jeans hung low on his hips and her eyes followed the very tempting trail of dark hair that went from his lower navel to below his jeans. She couldn't stop her mind from conjuring up images of what hid below.

Shaking her head to clear it, she glanced down at herself and her ruined clothes and decided a hot shower might help clear her mind. She flipped the lock on the front door, just in case there were more of him out there. Or in case whoever had done this to him came looking for him. She shivered at the thought. She made her way into the bathroom and locked the door behind her before stripping off her ruined clothes. Jumping into a steaming shower, her mind turned to thoughts of what she was going to do next.

Chapter Two

Caleb's head and hip were on fire. The shaking is what woke him from the deep sleep. He realized instantly that he was still laying on the cold tile just inside Billy's daughter's place.

Reaching over, he touched the fresh bandage over his wound and held in a groan. Sitting up slowly, he tore off his jacket and finished ripping off his ruined T-shirt. He was trying to peel off the bandage to get a better look at the wound, when he stopped cold as he heard talking in the next room. He pulled himself up quickly, only to grab hold of the back of the sofa as the room spun.

He didn't want to end up flat on his face again,

so he took a few deep breaths until his head settled back onto his shoulders.

The talking continued behind the door. He walked slowly over to it, but when he tried to turn the knob, he realized she'd locked him out. Who was she talking to? Was she calling the police?

He used his shoulder until the door gave way the second time he hit it. He'd used most of his strength and was just able to stop himself from falling on the floor as he entered the small bathroom.

She'd screamed when he'd pounded on the door, but now she stood there, behind a very sheer shower curtain, looking back at him. Her long dark hair flowed over her shoulders, which caused his eyes to travel further downwards. He could see a bright tattoo covering one of her shoulders that went all the way down to her mid-back. He had some ink himself—a small skull tattoo he'd gotten as an initiation into the Lone Outlaws—but nothing as impressive as hers. He couldn't quite see what it was through the curtain.

He blinked a few times as he realized he was standing there, gawking at her.

"Sorry," he started to say, only to watch her reach for a towel and almost slip and fall. He rushed forward to steady her just as she pushed him away. They both ended up falling backwards onto the floor directly in front of the sink.

He'd rolled slightly so that he took most of the fall and when his hip connected with the tile, a loud groan escaped as he felt the newly stitched skin open again.

"Damn it!" he cursed and closed his eyes as her wet, naked skin slid against his own. His mind was too focused on the pain shooting from his hip to notice how soft and wonderful she felt.

"What are you doing?" She tried to push herself up. His arms moved around her and held her still until he could catch his breath. "Let me go!" She squirmed in his arms.

"Hang on," he growled under his breath, needing just a moment to catch his breath.

"If you don't let me up this moment, I'm going to..."

He dropped his arms as his eyes slid closed.

He heard her moving around, most likely covering up that luscious body of hers. Then he heard her gasp.

"You're bleeding again."

"Yeah," he said without opening his eyes. "The reason I needed a moment."

"Why did you have to barge in here?" she said as she moved around the small room.

His head was still spinning, so he chose to keep his eyes closed tight.

"I thought..."—he took a few breaths as he felt her rip off the bandages— "you were calling someone."

"So?" she demanded as her fingers brushed over the torn stitches.

"You promised." His eyes finally opened. She was leaning over him, her long dark hair dripping down on him. She'd wrapped a bright yellow terry-cloth robe around herself. The color made her tan skin glow even more.

"I promised not to call the police or an ambulance." Her tone told him that she was annoyed at having to stitch him up again. "Not that I wouldn't call someone else."

"Did you?" His question seemed to stop her. Her fingers stilled over his skin as her blue eyes met his. He could see sadness in them and felt a need to find out what had caused it.

Finally, she seemed to decide on answering him and shook her head from side to side slowly.

"No, I tend to talk to myself when I'm harboring what I can only assume is a fugitive."

"I'm not wanted." He cringed a little at the lie.

"Right." The tone of her voice told him she knew.

"By the police." His eyes met hers. "Honest."

She stopped for a moment and then nodded. "Fair enough." He lay back as she finished sewing him up.

"Willa." He started to say something, anything to

reassure her.

"Don't call me that." He watched her eyes narrow with a little anger.

"Sorry, it's just..." He shook his head and groaned as she placed another clean bandage over the wound.

"Listen..." She leaned back. "I don't know how you knew my father, but it's clear—"

Just then there was a knock at the front door. Every muscle in his body tensed as he jumped up and pushed her behind him. His mind raced with a million ways they could escape the tiny apartment.

"What?" She tried to stand up, only to have him hold her still. "It's probably my..."

"No," he growled, thinking it was Al or Tony. What had he done? He'd led the two men to the one place he swore he'd never go. "Do you have a car?" he asked, rushing over and reaching for his ruined T-shirt.

"No." She stopped his hands. "Yes, I mean, I have a car, but don't put that thing on."

"Willow?" They stopped when a female voice called out from the other side of the front door.

"It's my sister," she whispered.

His body relaxed a bit. She walked into the front room and he followed her.

She'd stopped in front of the tile floor, covered

with his blood. "I'll get rid of her." She nodded for him to stand behind the door.

He watched her tuck her robe tighter around her front. When she opened the door, he saw her face soften.

"Hey." She leaned against the door so her sister wouldn't see into the apartment. "Sorry, I'm in the middle of a shower."

"Oh, I didn't mean to bother you, I just wanted to drop off the invitations."

"Yay!" Willow said and he could hear the excitement in her voice. "When are you sending them out?"

"Next week." Her sister's voice was a little higher pitched than Willow's was. "Can you believe it?"

Willow laughed. "What? That you're getting married or that you're marrying Cole Grayton?" She chuckled and the richness of her laughter melted something buried deep inside him.

"Both." Her sister's laughter didn't affect him in the same way. He stood between the door and the wall as the two women chatted for a few minutes. "Well, I'd better get going or I'll be late for work. See you tomorrow." He watched as Willow leaned in and hugged her sister.

When she finally shut the door, his knees almost gave way.

"Thanks," he said.

"For?" She leaned against the door and glanced at him. Her eyes moved over his chest, then zeroed in on the white bandage above his hip.

"For not telling her about me." His eyes met hers.

"Why did I do that?" She leaned her head against the door. "Who are you hiding from?" Her eyes moved to his once more.

His head was spinning and he doubted he had the strength to stand much longer. What he needed was a warm meal, a hot shower, and a bed.

"Later." He pushed off from the wall and started to pick up his ruined shirt again.

"Don't." She interrupted him. "I have a clean shirt that should fit you." She walked around the blood-covered tile and disappeared into the back room. When she came out again, he was on his hands and knees, using the dish towel to clean up his blood. He thought he would make himself useful and couldn't imagine forcing her to clean up all that blood herself.

"You don't have to do that," she said. She'd changed into a dark gray sweatshirt and tight black leggings that hugged every curve. He felt his mouth go dry knowing he'd seen what was underneath it all.

She set a pile of clothes for him on the sofa. "Why don't you go clean yourself up while I finish that."

He took his time standing up, and then nodded as

he grabbed the clothes and disappeared into the bathroom.

"Caleb?" Her voice stopped him from shutting the door. "Keep your bandage clean and dry."

He nodded his head again and shut the door between them.

Leaning his forehead against the cool wood of the door, he took a few cleansing breaths to try and stop the world from spinning.

Why hadn't she told her sister he was there?

A better question was; why did he get the hint that she trusted him?

Willow watched Caleb disappear into her bathroom and wondered why she'd hidden his presence from her sister. Maybe it was because she knew Wendy hated everything to do with their father.

She thought about her actions as she quickly cleaned up the blood and tossed his torn and bloody shirt into the trash can. Then she pulled out the fixings for grilled cheese sandwiches and potato soup.

When Caleb walked out of her bathroom again, he was wearing an old pair of Jake's shorts and one of his forgotten T-shirts. The shirt was too small and tight on Caleb, which only accented all those gorgeous muscles she'd been admiring since he'd fallen in her doorway.

"Feeling better?" she asked as she watched his movements. She could tell he was in pain and weak from the loss of blood.

"Much." His eyes were glued to the sandwich and soup she'd set down on the table.

"Sit, eat. You'll feel better after you get something in you." She held out the chair for him.

"Why are you doing this?" His eyes moved to hers. She could see confusion there.

"I'm not one-hundred percent sure myself." She walked over and poured herself a bowl of soup, then sat across from him at her small table.

He continued watching her.

"Eat." She scooped up a spoonful and started eating. He quickly followed suit.

"Thank you," he said once his bowl and sandwich were gone.

"Are you going to tell me who did this to you?" She leaned back in her chair and watched him.

He rolled his shoulders and rested his elbows on the table. He was looking pale and very tired.

"I guess you can say, in a roundabout way, it's your father's fault that I'm here. He's the reason I'm alive and the reason I was shot."

"Shot?" She sat up. "I thought you were stabbed." She looked towards his side again.

He shook his head. "I'm lucky it just grazed me." He ran his hand over his hip.

"How is it my father's fault?"

"Lone Outlaws, the bike gang he was in."

"My father never talked to me about it." Willow sighed and tucked her legs up tight to her chest.

He nodded. "I'm sure you were too young."

Her eyebrows shot up. "And you weren't?"

He smiled and for the first time since he'd barged in, she felt a shiver of fear race down her spine.

She watched his eyes go darker. "I was never young," he grunted.

They sat in silence for a while. "What happened tonight?" she finally asked.

"I've been running from my past too long." He leaned back and closed his eyes. "It finally caught up with me."

"I don't understand. What has that got to do with my father?"

"He's the reason they're trying to kill me."

She shook her head, not understanding.

"I'm too tired to go into it right now. Any chance I can crash here?" His eyes moved over to the sofa.

She thought about it. She had the next few days

off and had planned on spending her time enjoying herself with friends. But curiosity was getting the better of her and she really wanted to know more.

It wasn't as if she didn't trust him. Something in his eyes told her that he wasn't a rapist or a killer. Actually, it was kind of weird, but the only thing she could see in his dark eyes was pain, and she didn't think it only had to do with his physical wounds.

"I'll get you a blanket." She moved to stand up, but his fingers wrapped around her wrist, stopping her.

"You shouldn't let me stay." His eyes were focused on her fingers.

"I think I'm old enough to make my own decisions." She waited until he dropped her wrist. "Besides, I want to make sure you don't open those stitches again." She smiled down at him.

His eyes searched hers and when he nodded, she walked into her bedroom to retrieve an extra pillow and blanket.

He had moved the dishes into the sink and was laying on her small sofa when she came back into the room.

"I'm sorry about your dad," he said when she handed him the blanket and pillow.

"It was years ago." She tried to blow off the pain that always came when she thought about all the lost time with him.

35

His hand once again reached up to stop her from moving away. "If it wasn't for your dad, I'm pretty sure I would have been lying in a gutter long ago."

She had so many questions but could see that he'd run out of energy. "Tomorrow," she promised and he seemed to understand her since he gave her a slight nod.

"Goodnight," she whispered as she shut the lights off and moved into her own room.

She leaned against her door for a moment, trying to rationalize what she was doing. She was thankful that Wendy had been too distracted with her wedding invitations to wonder why she hadn't asked her in, even for a moment.

Her sister's life had taken a complete turn in the last year. She was excited for Wendy and Cole. Really she was. For the first time in her sister's life, Willow could see that Wendy was completely happy.

But she knew that Wendy was against anything that had to do with their father. If Wendy knew that Willow was harboring a friend of their father's... Willow shivered and pushed off from the doorway to crawl into bed. She lay there, trying to figure out how she could keep her sister from finding out about Caleb.

After almost an hour of staring at the ceiling, she tried reading for a while, but the mystery book held little interest since there was a bigger mystery sleeping in her living room. Turning over, she shut off her lamp and dreamed about the last time she had seen her father.

When she woke, the room was flooded with light. Willow wasn't normally a late sleeper, but on her days off, she forced her mind and body to stay shut down for a few extra hours. Glancing over at the clock, she realized there were still a few minutes of sleep she could get in.

Then her mind sharpened and she remembered Caleb in her living room.

Jumping up from the bed, she raced to the door, and slowly opened it just a crack. It was darker in the living room than her bedroom, since the curtains had been pulled shut last night. But she could just make out a large form covered with her blanket on the sofa.

She shut the door lightly and pulled on a fresh pair of jeans and a blouse. Finger combing her hair, she thought about sneaking into the bathroom and applying some makeup before checking on him.

Feeling more alive, she walked into the living room and cracked open the curtains so some light hit the sofa.

Caleb had removed Jake's shirt and was only wearing the shorts. She watched his massive chest rise and fall with each breath. One of his arms was thrown over his head and his other was half falling off the sofa as his bare feet hung over the other end.

His bandage was still covering his wound, but

she could see he'd bled through it again. It would need to be changed first thing. Walking over, she sat next to him and reached for the bandage, only to have the hand that was above him fly out and hold her wrist tight.

"What?" His dark eyes traveled all around the semi-dark room.

"It's okay; I just need to change your bandage." She glanced down at his fingers wrapped around her wrist.

"Sorry." He leaned back and rested his head down once more.

There were dark circles under his eyes and his skin looked translucent.

Reaching up, she touched his forehead and gasped. "You've got a fever." She jumped up and grabbed the bottle of medicine she'd tried to give him the night before. "Here." She handed him two pills and a glass of water.

His eyes opened and glared at her.

"I can be stubborn too." She tilted her head and waited until he reached up and took the pills from her.

Chapter Three

His mind was foggy and he was in more pain than he'd been in last night. How was that even possible?

Willow stood over him, her long dark hair tied back from her face, making him realize just how utterly beautiful she was. Her blue eyes showed worry and, yes, stubbornness.

Leaning up a little, he reached for the pills and water without another word. Then he watched her clean and switch out his bandages. Her teal-painted fingernails scraped his skin, sending shivers of awareness spiking over every nerve.

39

His fingers reached out and touched the tips of her hair, which almost brushed his elbow. "You used to be blonde." His mind had been playing over the one image he'd seen of the two girls, years ago.

She frowned down at him. "How did…" She shook her head and went back to her task. "I'm sure my father showed you many pictures."

He shook his in return. "Just the one." He remembered seeing the two girls locked around their father in the happiest family moment he'd ever witnessed.

Her dark eyebrows shot up. "I'd like to hear more, but I think you need some additional rest. I'll make you some tea."

He made a face. He didn't like tea. What he wanted was a strong shot of whiskey to get him back on his feet.

"You may not like tea, but you'll drink at least a cup of it for me." She moved away from the sofa, taking his dirty bandages with her. "I didn't see signs of infection," she said as she moved around the small kitchen. "That's a good sign, but I'll want to…" He must have zoned out while she continued to chat with herself as she prepared his tea. He woke when she shook his shoulders.

"Sorry," he mumbled and tried to sit up. He stopped when he noticed that she was frowning down at him.

"You've been out for almost four hours." Her hand went to his forehead where a cool washcloth

40

covered his eyebrows. "I tried to wake you." Her frown increased as she shook her head from side to side. "I was so scared. I didn't know what to do." He noticed then that her hands shook when they removed the washcloth from his forehead.

Reaching out, he took her hands in his to steady them.

"Willa?" His voiced sounded so far away. His eyelids felt extra heavy. "Don't be scared. I'm okay." He reached up to run his fingers through her hair as he shut his eyes once more.

"No, you're not. Your fever is getting worse." He felt her cool hands on his face. He could tell she'd laid another cloth on his chest, but so far, all he could feel was the heat coming from the core of his body. "You need a hospital." Her words made it past the fog in his brain. Opening his eyes, he took her hand in his and pulled her close until his eyes could focus on her face.

"You promised." It came out as a growl.

"And I intend on keeping my promise. But—"

"No!" he barked out, stopping her next words.

"Caleb, I can't sit back and watch you die."

"I'll be fine. I just need some rest." His eyes slid close. He didn't even realize she was still pressed fully against his chest. All he knew was that for the first time since he'd lain down on the small sofa, he was finally comfortable.

41

Willow was squished against Caleb's heated skin, his fingers still tangled in her loose locks. Her hands were wedged between them, but for the first time in hours, he was breathing normally.

She'd made him soup instead of tea, but when she'd walked over to wake him up, he hadn't budged. At all. She'd even shook him as hard as she dared, fearing she'd open his wound again.

But his dark lashes had stayed closed and his breathing had been labored. She'd paced, worried, and then covered his burning flesh with cool washcloths, which had seemed to help.

She hadn't even realized how much she'd worn herself out worrying about him until she felt herself relax against his chest. Soon, her breathing matched his and she allowed her eyes to close for just a moment.

Her cell phone ringing jolted her awake a few minutes later. Untangling herself from his arms wasn't an easy task. Finally, she rushed over to the table and answered her sister's call with a whisper.

"Were you still asleep?" Wendy's voice was drowned out in a sea of shouts.

"No," she whispered and decided to move into the bedroom so she could talk normal.

"Then why are you whispering?" Wendy asked.

"I'm not," she said as she shut her door and leaned back against it. "You're just in a really loud bar."

"True, the game is on."

"Game?" Willow rubbed her forehead and thought about taking an aspirin herself.

"Yeah, remember? You, me, my fiancé and his family... Pizza, beer, game." Wendy sighed. "You forgot."

Then she remembered. "I'm sorry, I woke up sick." She hated lying to her sister, but there was some truth behind it. Her head was starting to pound from all the worry.

"I'm sorry. Do you need me to stop by?"

"No!" She almost shouted it and then took a couple deep breaths. "I wouldn't want to get you sick. Not with all the wedding planning you still have to do."

Wendy chuckled. "The wedding isn't for two months."

"I'll be okay. Really. I'm going to spend the weekend in, watching reruns."

"Okay, but if you need anything..."

"Thanks. Have fun watching the game."

There were some muffled noises, and then her sister came back on the phone. "Cole and his family say hi and hope you feel better."

"Tell them thanks." She sighed and closed her eyes as she shut her phone off.

There was a light knock on the door, causing her to jump.

"Everything okay?" Caleb asked from the other side of the door.

She swung the door open and looked up into his face. He was leaning against her door jam, still pale and half-naked, but his eyes actually looked clearer.

"Are you okay?" She leaned in and felt his forehead.

"Much better," he said as she watched him sway a little.

She reached over and took his shoulders, making him walk back towards the sofa. He stopped dead in his tracks. His eyes focused on his small bed area.

"I'll sit anywhere but there. That thing is uncomfortable." He rolled his shoulders slightly.

She nodded towards the kitchen table, and he followed her to sit down.

"I can heat some soup."

"Sounds good." He leaned back in the chair.

She busied herself heating a pan of chicken noodle soup and threw a loaf of French bread in the oven to heat up. When she sat down next to him, she realized she hadn't eaten yet that day.

"This is good," he said between bites. "Better than that stuff from last night."

She nodded. "My neighbor brought it over earlier." She took another bite. "Mrs. Kingston's daughter died a few years ago. Since then, she's doted on me."

He finished his soup and bread and leaned back. "It's strange, but I could use another shower and a nap." He shook his head and she watched him roll his shoulders once more.

She tried not to watch his muscles flex with each movement. But he was still sitting across from her in just Jake's old shorts.

"I could see if I have a larger T-shirt?" she blurted out. She watched his eyebrows rise up a little. Then he looked down and frowned.

"I didn't want to get blood on your boyfriend's stuff," he mumbled.

"He's not... We're no longer together." She couldn't connect with his eyes, so instead, she watched his hands as he picked up his bowl.

"You don't have to clean up." She quickly stood to grab the bowl and spoon from him, but he moved it up high above his head.

"I may have never had a family or a place of my own, but I know how to clean up after myself."

She dropped her hands to her side and frowned at him.

"You didn't have a family?"

He blinked a few times and just looked back at her.

"The bike gang was my only family." He set the bowl in the sink. "The gang and your dad." He walked back and sat down at the table once more.

She set her bowl next to his and then went and sat across from him, tucking her legs underneath herself and wrapping her arms around them.

"And?"

He signed and looked at her. "Let's just say, I know exactly why they want me dead. Actually..." He tilted his head and squinted his eyes slightly. "Tony mentioned something about taking me back to pay. So, I'm pretty sure there are others wanting to pay me back as well."

She leaned closer and bumped her knees against the table. Reaching out, she steadied it. "Back? Back where?" She waited.

"Home." The word came out in a sarcastic half laugh.

"Where is home?" she asked.

"I have no home." His voice had grown darker.

She shook her head, not understanding.

"Home base for the Lone Outlaws," he said and she shivered at the name of her father's motorcycle gang. He noticed and turned his lips upward in an almost sneer. "You should fear them." He nodded slightly. "I do." He closed his eyes and rested his head back. "Home base is just outside of Miami."

She frowned. "Dad always said…" When he sat up and watched her, she shook her head and stopped talking.

"What?" He leaned on the table, trying to get closer.

"Nothing. It's nothing." She rested back.

"Willa, if you know something."

She stood up quickly and looked down at him. "I told you, don't call me that. Only he called me that." She walked over to the sink and started washing the dishes that had piled up. She needed something to do with her hands.

"I'm sorry." His voice was right behind her. When his hands rested on her shoulders, she jumped a little and spun around. Her wet, soapy hands splashed on his chest.

She glared up at him. For some reason, the fact that this stranger knew more about her father than she did really set her off.

"Tell me more." She turned back to finish the dishes, feeling the need to finish her task. "How did you meet him?"

He crossed his arms over his chest and leaned against the countertop next to her. "I delivered a package to him."

She glanced at him from the corner of her eyes.

"A package?"

"Drugs," he said flatly. "To him and the gang."

"How old were you?" She was beginning to doubt his story. After all, she'd been two months' shy of her tenth birthday when her father had died. There was no way he was more than five years older than her.

"A week after my thirteenth birthday." He turned his head and looked out into her living room. "Back then, they had a standing rule." He closed his eyes and she could tell he was remembering. "No messengers survived."

"What?" She almost dropped the dish she was drying.

"Like I said, you should fear them."

She shook her head. "I find it hard to believe that my father…"

He took the dish and the towel from her and took her shoulders into his hands. "No, like I said, your father *saved me*."

"I don't…"

"Willa… Willow, sit down." He started to move them towards the sofa, but she stopped him.

"Are you telling me that my father was friends with killers?"

"No, what I'm telling you is that he was a member of a gang who were—are—killers."

She reached up and touched her forehead, feeling even more of a headache spread. "I'm not following you."

He let out a deep breath and then nodded to the sofa. "Sit."

She crossed her arms over her chest in defiance, but she knew that the only way to get the whole story from him was to give him what he wanted. Walking over, she sat near the end of the sofa and tucked her feet up underneath her.

She thought he would come and sit next to her, but instead, he walked over to her sliding doors and peeked out the heavy curtains. He stood there for a few moments while she waited. He was trying her patience. She was just about to jump up and demand that he start talking, when he turned around.

"I was born in a small town just outside of Vegas. My mother was a whore and from the moment she conceived me, she did everything in her power to get rid of me. Short of murder. Needless to say, when I was nine, I was picked up by the police, and she took that as a sign that I should be on my own. I was doing okay, living on the streets of Vegas, until the night a guy on a bike asked if I wanted to make a thousand bucks just for delivering a package."

She tensed, knowing what was coming.

"Well, as you can guess it, it was too good to be true. From what I understand, the group liked to bring kids into the gang. If they said no… Well, you can guess why they had me deliver clear out in the desert."

She shivered and hugged her legs closer to her. "My father?" Her voice was low as a million images flashed into her mind.

"No. Or so he said, and the years I was with him, I never saw…" He shook his head. "No."

She took a deep breath and released it. Well, at least there was that, she thought as she closed her eyes.

"Hey." His voice was right in front of her. He'd moved across the room without her even knowing it. Now he was on his knees in front of her. His hands reaching out for hers. "Your father was a good guy. Honest."

She swallowed the disgust that had lodged in her throat and nodded. "Go on."

He moved to sit next to her. "Billy took me in, like I was his own. He taught me things. Everything actually." He chuckled, the sound sending shivers down her back. It wasn't fear this time, but something else she couldn't quite put her finger on. "Then, when he left…" He turned his eyes back to the patio door. "I left too."

"Where did you go? What did you do?" she asked.

He turned sad eyes to her and said, "Everywhere, anything… Places to see, people to meet."

Chapter Four

There was so many things that Caleb had learned over the years of being on his own. The most important one was how to read people. Right now, however, he couldn't tell anything about Willow. She'd crossed her arms over her chest and was staring out towards the patio doors.

"What happened to the gang after my father left?"

He shrugged his shoulders. "Some went to jail." He avoided her eyes. "Some disappeared."

She was frowning at him again. The small crease

between her eyebrows was calling out to him. He wanted to reach up and rub the spot until it went away.

"But you said that they found you and want you dead?"

He nodded. "A few months back, I'd heard that some of them had gotten out of jail and were banding back together again." She shook her head and he knew she didn't understand. "Sounds like they're looking to get everyone back together and dish up some paybacks." He avoided her eyes once more.

"Payback for what?"

"Who do you think put them away?"

"You were just a kid." She sat up a little. "Surely they don't mean…"

He nodded, interrupting her. "Lone Outlaws is for life. You don't snitch on your family," he said in a drone-like voice.

"They aren't your family." He turned his head and looked at her. He knew his eyes and face said everything. "What are you going to do?"

He tilted his head. The fact was, he had several plans. None of them had involved him getting shot in the back alley of a Chinese restaurant.

Remembering, he walked over to pick up his jacket from the chair she'd set it in. Reaching into the inside pocket, he came up empty. "Where is it?" He checked the other pockets.

"What?" she asked from the sofa.

Instead of answering, he frantically searched his jacket then looked in his jeans.

"There was a small brown package," he said. "Did you see it?" he demanded.

She shook her head as her eyes grew bigger. He watched her ball up tight as she sat on the sofa. Taking a few deep breaths, he closed his eyes and tried to remember the last time he'd had the key to his next step.

"The alley," he blurted out.

"What?" she asked, causing his eyes to open. Racing around, he grabbed up her ex-boyfriend's shirt and his jeans and boots. Without answering her, he walked into the bathroom and shut himself inside, changing quickly into his jeans and the borrowed shirt.

When he came back out, he was surprised to see her blocking his exit. She had pulled on a jacket and boots and had her arms crossed over her chest.

"You're not leaving me here."

He laughed. "I'm not taking you with me."

She tilted her head. "You haven't finished telling me about my father."

He frowned. "You know enough." He took her shoulders and moved her aside, but she moved back in front of the door as she held up a set of keys.

53

"I have a car." She smiled.

When he reached up to take the keys from her, she quickly tucked them inside her jacket. "I'm going." She grabbed her purse and opened the door for him.

"Fine, but you're staying in the car." He stepped outside and realized it was once again raining.

"Here." She held out a bright pink umbrella.

He chuckled. "I'd rather get wet."

She smiled slightly as she looked up at him. "Not man enough to wear pink?" Her eyes laughed at him, so he took her challenge and reached out for the umbrella, holding it for her as she locked her apartment door.

They sprinted to her car, a little silver Toyota Prius.

"This isn't a car," he said after getting in the passenger side.

"It's a perfectly good car. Gets over forty-five miles to the gallon and it's a hybrid. I'm saving the planet every time I drive to work."

He shook his head. "You're one of those—" He cut off when she gave him a dirty look. Turning his head, he chose to remain silent as she backed out of the parking lot.

"Where to?"

"Chinese place by the pier."

"PJ's?" She looked at him and waited.

He shrugged. "I didn't stop to read the sign as the bullets flew by my head."

He watched her close her eyes and take a deep breath. Then she opened them and focused as she turned towards the right. At least she was headed in the right direction.

"How are you feeling?" she asked as she drove.

"My side is still on fire, but not as bad as it was earlier." He looked down and touched the bandage. "I think your stitches are holding."

"You never told me exactly who is after you." She glanced over at him. "Or why."

He focused on where she was going for a moment and decided a half-truth would be best.

"Al and Tony. I spotted the two of them in Miami." He looked over at her as he talked. "I was working in a night club." Shaking his head, he turned his eyes back to the road as the rain splashed over her small car. "Anyway, they paid me a visit." His ribs still hurt from the initial punch Tony had given him before he'd blocked the rest of the hits. "So, I took off."

"Did you come here looking for my father? Did you think he could help you?" she asked as she stopped for a four-way intersection.

"No." His voice grew soft. "I knew he couldn't help. I wasn't planning on talking to him."

"Then…" She turned her shoulders towards him. "Why did you come here? To Surf Breeze?" She glanced around. "We're not exactly a great place to hide out."

He chuckled. "I figured that out last night." He rubbed his side as the car started moving again.

"Why did you come here then?"

"I had something I needed to deliver back to him." He thought about the importance of the contents in the package.

"What?" she asked as she parked in a spot near the mouth of the alley behind the Chinese restaurant.

He turned and looked at her. "Proof he needed in order for him to be free forever."

She frowned at him. "But he's dead."

Caleb nodded. "That's no excuse."

Something in Caleb's voice caused a shiver to run down her arms. Throwing the car into park, she wrapped her arms around herself and thought about turning up the heater.

"Stay here." He started to get out of the car, but stopped and looked back towards her, his dark eyes meeting hers until she felt like blinking and looking away. "Lock the doors and don't talk to anyone." He waited until she nodded, then quickly disappeared down the alley.

She noticed that he'd left her pink umbrella behind and shook her head slightly. After flipping the door locks, she reached for the heater and turned it to full blast.

Hot summer days were taking forever to get here. It seemed like only a few months ago she was begging for a little relief from the heat. Now, however, she couldn't wait for the few weeks of rain and cold winds to be over.

Her eyes were glued to the mouth of the alley, waiting for any signs of Caleb to return. Seconds turned into minutes. The sun slowly sank behind the buildings, giving the dark street an even more dangerous feeling.

After half an hour, the rain eased up and she decided to shut off her car to save what little gas was left in her tank.

She was getting really worried and a few minutes later, she made up her mind. Grabbing her pink umbrella just in case it started raining again, she locked her car and headed into the alley.

There were six small shops, including the restaurant, along the street back. Large trash bins lined the left side of the alley. On the right stood empty pallets stacked higher than her head below the dim alley lights.

The rain had done a good job cleaning the normally dirty backstreet. Still, she couldn't stop the shivering or the feeling that she should have stayed in the car like Caleb had asked her.

When she reached the mouth of the alley, she stopped and looked around. Caleb was nowhere to be found.

"Can I help you?" someone said from behind her. Spinning around as she squealed, she held her pink umbrella tighter to her chest.

An elderly gentleman stood under a bright light at the back door of one of the shops. The door was propped open with an old chair. There was a bucket full of cigarette butts sitting beside it.

"Sorry, I didn't mean to frighten you," he said as he threw a cigarette butt into the full bucket.

She took a deep breath. "It's okay." Taking a few steps back, she turned to go.

"Are you looking for something?" he asked, stopping her.

"Um." She glanced around once more, remembering what Caleb had told her. "No. I just turned down the wrong street. Thank you." She started to turn again.

"Well, I was just wondering, because I found this on my doorstep this morning." He pulled out a small brown package and held it up. "Thought whoever dropped it might come back looking for it. We don't tend to get mail dropped around here. Our mail boxes are out front of the stores, you see." The older man waved the package.

From her spot a few feet away, she could see her father's name clearly written in dark ink on the front.

"Yes." She took a step closer. "It's mine. My father's," she corrected.

His eyebrows shot up. "Thought so." He smiled, showing off a space where his front teeth should have been.

She hesitated for a moment as he held it out towards her. "Well, go ahead. I won't bite." He smiled even bigger, showing the empty mouth once more.

She smiled and reached out for it, her eyes totally focused on the prize.

When her fingers wrapped around the crisp brown paper package, she quickly tucked it close to her and took a giant step back.

"Thank you…"

"John." The older man smiled again. "My wife and I own the doll shop." He nodded to the brick building.

"Thank you, John." She turned to go, only to see Caleb striding towards her quickly.

"I thought I told you to stay put," he growled as he reached for her, his eyes moving over the older man. When his fingers wrapped around her upper arm, she allowed him to pull her back down the alley towards her car.

"You've been gone for—"

"That doesn't matter," he interrupted. "When I tell you to stay put, I expect you to—"

Willow yanked her arm free. "What? Obey?" She hissed it out and took a step backwards.

She saw him swallow some of his anger and then looked closer to see fear behind those dark eyes.

"Is this what you were looking for?" She held up the small package.

His eyes opened wide as he looked. "Where did you…?" He quickly shook his head and glanced around. "I'm driving." He held out his hand for her to give him the keys.

"Like hell." She started to cross her arms over her chest, but then realized she still had her umbrella and the bundle in her hands.

He wiggled his fingers. "Willow, let me drive so you can read that." He nodded to the parcel.

She thought about it and then nodded and handed him her keys.

"Get in." He walked over to passenger side and opened the door for her, then moved around and got behind the wheel.

She tucked her umbrella under her feet and reached for her seat belt just as he pulled out of the parking spot.

"Well, go ahead." He nodded to the package. "Open it."

She ran her fingers over her father's name and slowly turned the small box over and tore it open.

There, in her hands, was her father's old journal. The one she could always remember him having on him. Every time he'd visit, he would tuck the small binder into her mother's jewelry box on Willow's dresser for safekeeping. She was never allowed to look inside it, but had snuck a few glances. It had been full of boring names and dates, so naturally, as a child, it held no special interest.

Now, as she opened it, she felt tears sting her eyes when she recognized her father's handwriting. There was a long row of dates, numbers, and initials on each page. The meaning of it was beyond her comprehension.

"What is this?" she asked, glancing up. She realized that he'd driven them to the outskirts of town.

"It's your and your sister's insurance."

"I don't understand." She leaned on the door and blinked a few times as she flipped from page to page. More dates, more initials, more numbers. None of it made sense.

"Check out the bottom of the last page," he said as he pulled into a gas station.

She flipped back and stared at the short line on the last page. It was written in dark ink and she couldn't stop staring at it the entire time he was filling up her tank. When he finally got back into the car, she found her voice.

Places to go, people to meet.

"He always said that line to me. But what does this book have to do with my sister and me? What does this book even mean?"

"I don't know. He never told me anything other than it would assure his freedom and to hold onto it. It could mean nothing in particular. But to your father…" He started her car again. "It meant everything." He pulled out of the gas station.

"Where are we going?" She finally looked around and realized he was still pointing the car out of town.

"I need to check on something." His eyes were focused on the road and she could tell he was hiding something from her.

"Where?" She tucked the journal into her purse.

"A few miles outside of town."

"I thought… How long have you been around here?"

His fingers gripped the steering wheel. "I've been hiding out in a little hotel a few miles away for a few weeks."

She felt her heart skip. "Why?"

His eyes moved over to her. "I had to make sure it was safe."

She remained silent for a while. He pulled over and stopped in front of one of the scariest looking hotels she'd ever seen.

"You stayed here?" She shivered, dreading seeing what the inside looked like.

"It's not as bad as it looks." His eyes roamed over the small building that looked like it was falling in. "Stay put." He started to get out but stopped and turned back to her. "This time I mean it." Just the sound of his voice told her that he was even more serious than before.

"Fine," she said, trying to smile back at him. It probably ended up looking more like a scowl than a smile, since his eyes narrowed slightly.

She watched him get out, glance around the small parking lot, then head towards one of the bright green doors with the number four hanging upside down on it.

He disappeared inside and she leaned back in her seat to wait. She watched a young couple arguing as they walked out of the door next to his and continue to argue as they jumped into an old beat-up truck and drive off.

She remembered always fighting with Jake. Their relationship had been like a ticking time bomb. She was never sure when an argument was going to start or when he was going to get up and walk out. She'd hated not feeling like her sister and Cole did.

When she looked at them, there was no doubt that they were one-hundred percent committed to one another. It was strange, seeing her sister with the surfing playboy. Cole was easily the best-looking man she'd ever met. Well, maybe not anymore, she thought as she looked towards the green door with the upside-down four.

She smiled. Caleb was something to look at. Her mouth actually had watered when she'd first gotten a look at his chest and that six-pack he'd been hiding under his ruined shirt.

She didn't want to admit the reason it had taken her so long to stitch him up was because she couldn't bear to leave a large scar on his perfect skin.

Just then, her cell phone rang, causing her to jump. Reaching down, she yanked it out of her purse and noticed her sister's picture pop up on the screen.

"Hey," she answered, her eyes staying on the green door as she waited for Caleb.

"How are you feeling?"

"Much better." She closed her eyes for a moment, wishing she didn't have to lie to her sister.

"I stopped by your place after the game, but I guess you're out."

"Yeah, I had a few errands to run."

"Anything I can help with? I mean, if you're not feeling—"

"No, I'm fine. I'm just running to the store. You know…" She bit her bottom lip as she watched Caleb walk out of the door with a large black bag thrown over his shoulders. He'd changed his clothes from Jake's small T-shirt and was wearing a dark gray T-shirt and a pair of worn faded jeans.

He looked more dangerous than he had the night before, trying to get into her apartment. He tossed the bag into the back of her car and got back behind the wheel.

"Helloooo." Her sister's voice sounded loud in her ear. She'd completely forgotten she was still on the phone with Wendy.

"Sorry." She shook her head clear of what watching Caleb did to her.

"Are you sure you're okay?" She could hear worry in her sister's voice.

"Yes, I'm fine. I'll talk to you tomorrow." She was relieved when Wendy hung up a few seconds later.

"Everything okay?" he asked as he started the car.

"Yeah, just my sister."

"You two sound close," he said as he backed out.

"Not really." She shook her head. "Wendy is eight years older." She sighed remembering all the years she felt nothing but resentment towards her big sister. "Honestly, it wasn't until the hurricane last year that things changed."

He glanced over at her, his eyebrows up in question.

"She was hurt." A spike of fear that still lingered every time she remembered the day jumped inside her again.

"What happened?"

"She was hit with flying debris and lost her eyesight for a while."

"You must have been scared."

She nodded. "Since then, things have changed between us." He waited, and she could tell he wanted more information.

"I always wanted a brother or sister," he said, surprising her. She watched his fingers grip the steering wheel more tightly. "A normal family." He sighed, and she could feel the pain he was hiding, had hidden inside all his life.

"You know; Wendy was my only mother figure. Actually, since our father wasn't around very much, she played both roles."

He frowned as he looked at her. "What happened to your mother?"

She'd gotten over the fear of telling everyone where her mother had been during her childhood years ago. "Jail," she blurted out as she shrugged her shoulders, wanting to change the conversation. "Wendy's mother died before I was born. Shortly after having me, my mother was locked up and"— she sighed and looked out her window— "she never came back."

She was shocked to feel his hand reach for hers. His fingers were much bigger than hers, rougher too. Just his light touch sent awareness rushing through her.

"I'm sorry." His eyes locked with hers for a split second.

"Still, I had Wendy." She smiled, swallowing the pain of the loss.

He nodded and dropped her hand as he turned the car into her apartment building's parking lot.

"What now?" she asked after he turned off her car and handed her the keys.

"Now, I leave town." He turned slightly towards her. "Keep that journal safe."

She shook her head. "I still don't understand."

He sighed. "When I make my next move, you will."

"You still haven't told me what it all means."

He leaned back in the seat and glanced around the small parking lot.

"Come in," she blurted out. For some reason, she found it hard to curb her tongue when she was around him. She made a mental note to try harder to control those sporadic urges to bark things out. "I mean, so we can talk further…" She felt her face heat, so she turned away and started opening her door.

"Willow." His hand on her arm stopped her movement. "I can't stick around. The longer I'm here, the more you and your sister are in danger."

She swallowed hard and then nodded slightly. "Let me check your bandage and give you something hot to eat, and then… we can talk." She waited until he finally took a deep breath and nodded.

Chapter Five

What was he doing? He should be on the next bus out of town, heading far away from the cozy town. Instead, he was sitting on Willow's uncomfortable sofa, watching her move around her small kitchen making grilled chicken sandwiches.

Just watching how she moved distracted him, once more. He'd been on the beach, watching her with the group of other workers all dressed alike as they put up the small enclosures to protect the sea turtles.

Caleb had been following Willow for days. Actually, not really following, since all he had to do was sit on the white sugar sand and pretend to stare out at the vast teal-blue waters of the Gulf of Mexico. He'd sat on the beach each day for almost an entire week, totally exposed to his enemies, just so he could watch her.

He'd been attracted to her instantly, and he'd never been one to deny his feelings towards women before. This time, however, it was different. He knew he could never act on his desire for her.

He kept telling himself that he'd wait until he'd seen Billy, so he didn't have to approach her. Then he'd give Billy the journal and move on. But every time he heard her laugh or watched her smile, something shifted inside him. Something told him to continue watching her instead of looking for her old man.

Actually, he'd found her sister, Wendy, first. She'd been easier to find than he'd imagined.

When he'd first come into town, he'd found her sisters' addresses in the phone book under W. Blake. He'd assumed it had to be William, her father.

He'd watched the sisters meet at the Boardwalk Bar and Grill where Wendy worked, then something had forced him to follow Willow home instead of sticking with the older sister. Maybe it was because Wendy always had a guy hanging a few feet away from her and he didn't want to run into problems. Besides, there was always a group of people around the blonde bartender.

Willow, on the other hand, was more of a loner. Like him. So he'd decided to watch her for a few days. Then he'd followed her as she worked and noticed how good she looked barefoot, her brightly colored toenails sinking into the sand as she dug into the soft earth. Some days, as she worked, her hair had been tied back from her face, other's she'd left it down, flowing in the soft breeze, making him wish more than anything that he could run his fingers through it.

His eyes moved to the soft locks now. She'd left her hair down and it lay in soft waves to the middle of her back. His eyes moved lower. She had one of the sexiest bodies he could remember seeing.

In the past five years, he'd worked so many odd jobs, he couldn't count them all. One of his favorites had been playing bouncer at nightclubs. Women came and went in small sexy outfits and always hung on him or begged him to let them into the high-profile clubs in Miami. Of course, he'd always oblige, if they made it worth his while.

Now, he was wondering what he'd have to do to get Willow to hang on his arm like that.

"Here." Her voice broke into his daydreams. "It's ready." She sat at the table and watched as he made his way to the chair.

"I could have helped. A few years back, I worked in a dive flipping burgers."

"I enjoy cooking. Even the simplest meals. Now,

71

dishes on the other hand are an entirely different matter." She smiled across the table at him.

"Had a job doing those, too." He remembered getting fired less than a week later because he hated it.

"Sounds like you've moved around a lot." He could hear the hint of excitement in her voice.

His eyes moved to hers. She was smiling at him; her blue eyes were sparkling with humor.

"I had to," he said, biting into the hot sandwich, not really tasting the food. Too much history flooded his mind as he thought about all the places—too many—he'd tried to fit into.

It seemed like all he'd been doing his whole life was trying to find one place to feel like he belonged. To date, he hadn't found that place. He wondered if he'd spend his entire life looking.

"To hide from the gang?" she asked, nibbling on her own food. His eyes zeroed in on the movement. Her lips were something he'd found himself staring at since the first time he'd seen her up close. The combination of her blue eyes with her pink lips made him struggle to keep his desire in check.

He blinked and focused on answering her instead of thinking about how soft those lips of hers would feel under his. He couldn't afford to let his guard down again. The pain in his side and hip reminded him of that every time he took a breath.

"At first, after I left the gang, it was because I

didn't know where I belonged." He remembered the many nights he'd slept in dives or on the streets, trying to figure out who he wanted to be. "I started out by going back to Vegas, but..." He shook his head and set his half-eaten sandwich back down. "I quickly realized that town had nothing more for me."

"Where did you go next?" she asked after finishing half her sandwich.

"California." He cringed inwardly at the memories. Of all the places he'd traveled, he'd felt the most like an outcast there. There were too many rich people, too many junkies... Too many damn people, period. "I got stuck in this hole of a place. I was working at a gas station near the corner of Hollywood and Vine. Then, one night, I woke up and decided to head east."

"No reason?" she asked, leaning closer.

He shrugged. "None that I could think of, other than a feeling I had to go."

"How did you end up in Miami?"

His eyes moved to hers and he knew this next part would get even more complicated. He must have been looking at her funny, because she tilted her head and crossed her arms over her chest in a stubborn move, showing him she wasn't going to back out of her line of questioning.

"Caleb, what aren't you telling me?"

He sighed and stood up, hiding the wince at the

streak of pain that shot down his leg. He walked back towards the sliding glass doors. He peeked out the heavy curtains into the darkness. The parking lot was empty of movement.

He'd been watching out for Al or Tony all day as they drove around, making sure they hadn't been followed on the short trip to the alley and to the motel he'd been catching a few hours of sleep each night at.

He could just make out the dark beach on the other side of a cluster of trees and wished he could spend the rest of his days watching Willow protect the wildlife.

"Hey." Her voice was right behind him. When her arm reached up and rested on his shoulder, he closed his eyes at the soft touch.

"I went to Miami because I was contacted by your father."

Willow's knees went weak. Caleb's hands took her shoulders, then his arms wrapped around her, pulling her close until his chest hit hers.

"Easy," he whispered next to her ear.

Her eyes refocused on his face. "I…" She shook her head, not understanding.

How could her father have contacted Caleb?

Why would he have even if he was still alive?

"No," she said to herself, not realizing she'd spoken out loud. "Wendy said… We spread his ashes at the beach." She remembered that day, crying so hard her sister had to carry her home.

She felt Caleb nod. "I knew instantly that it wasn't your father." He pulled back until she looked up into his eyes once more. "I was working and going to school in Atlanta." He chuckled and she could see a hint of anger behind his eyes. "I got a message to come to Miami as fast as possible" He dropped his arms from her and took a step back. Instantly she missed his warmth. "Then Agent Minster contacted me instead."

She felt her heart skip. "Agent…"

His eyes moved back to her. "You should sit down." He motioned towards the sofa. She followed him and sat down.

"That day, when your father left the gang, and I followed him…" He took a deep breath. "We left together and drove over a hundred miles to meet Agent Minster. From the US Marshall Services."

She waited. Nothing he was saying made sense. Her mind raced to the night her father had returned home for the last time. The night he'd been late and had come home long after they'd been asleep.

She nodded slightly, letting him know she was ready to hear more.

He sat next to her, close. His arm was brushing

hers and he'd twisted around so his shoulders faced hers, which caused their knees to be up against one others.

His eyes were glued to her hands. "Turns out your dad had decided long ago to turn state's evidence against the gang because of what they'd start doing a few years back. He'd spent years collecting everything he had." He closed his eyes, resting his head on the back of the sofa.

She watched his Adam's apple as he swallowed and enjoyed the cords of muscles in his neck. He leaned up and looked back into her eyes. "Your father and I testified against Ralphie, Corbin, Richard, and six other gang members thirteen years ago. Most of them are still serving life, but several, like Al and Tony, were released in the last year."

"My father..." She reached up and touched the side of her head. "What?" She couldn't voice her questions, and was thankful when he continued to tell her the story.

"Turns out that the Lone Outlaws were one of the top organized crime groups in the States back then. They were one of the primary drug suppliers in the Southeastern states. They had a successful drug run from Mexico into the States, one of the only ones back then that hadn't been shut down or turned over to the cartel. The FBI, Marshall's office, and several local law agencies had spent years trying to infiltrate the group. To stay under the radar, they had been supplying funds for several local political campaigns and law enforcement officers." His eyes closed briefly. "So, naturally, their influence had grown pretty high up over the years. They thought they were untouchable…"

"How does my father fit in all this?"

Caleb reached over and brushed a strand of her hair away from her cheek. When his hand remained near her, she fought the urge to push her face into it.

"He told me it was the day you were born. He couldn't be there, for you or your mother. He'd been sent on a task to help Corbin, the second in command, clean up the mess after he'd beaten his pregnant girlfriend up. They paid law officials and city employees off. Made sure the entire situation got swept under the rug, all with drug and blackmail money. Billy told me that the young girl had lost the baby the same day you were born." He shook his head and then reached up and brushed a tear from her cheek. She hadn't realized she'd been crying and, to be honest, didn't even know why.

Maybe it was the fact that her father, whom she'd sworn would be the only man she'd ever love, had been involved in such a gang. Maybe it was because her father had chosen to spend his time with men who would do such a thing instead of with Wendy and her.

Maybe her sister had been right all those years. Maybe they were better off without him around.

Jill Sanders

Chapter Six

*H*e didn't know what had changed in her, but all of a sudden, her eyes grew sad and distant. He'd seen the tears and each one that fell broke his heart even more. But now, her eyes were deeper blue than he'd seen before. Her bottom lip crumpled as her eyes closed.

"Hey." His voice was soft as he pulled her closer to him. "What's this all about?"

Her head rested on his shoulder as he ran his fingers through her dark locks.

"I never believed," she said into his shirt. "I

always thought…"

He heard a sniffle and wished more than anything that he could make her smile again.

"Wendy always said…" She mumbled something against his shoulder, but he couldn't make it out, so he leaned back, putting his hands on either side of her face, waiting until she looked up at him before he asked her to repeat her words.

"Wendy always told me that we were better off without him in our lives. That he was a deadbeat dad and he didn't deserve us."

He felt a kick to the chest. From the sounds of it, Billy hadn't been much of a father to his two daughters. But to Caleb, he'd been everything.

He'd been the man who had taught him right from wrong. Good from evil. Without Billy, Caleb would have ended up just like Al or Tony. Or worse, he would have been dead years ago.

How was he supposed to soothe her pain when he had nothing but gratitude towards the man that rescued him?

"Willa," he said, brushing a few strands that had stuck to her tears. "I didn't think…"

Before he could finish, she pushed up and brushed her lips against his. His mind shut off the second he felt the softness against him.

Her arms wrapped around his neck, holding him closer. He could feel her soft chest against his and needed to feel more of her. She pushed down until he fell backwards onto the sofa softly, with her covering him.

"Caleb." Her soft breath fell over his chin as she moaned his name. Just his name on her lips had him forgetting time and place. The sweet sound vibrated something deep inside him. Something beyond basic. Almost animalistic. His desire spiked faster and harder than he'd ever experienced before. Before he knew what he was doing, he'd moved until she was below him, her legs wrapped around his hips as he pushed his desire against her core while his lips covered hers. Harder and faster, his kisses were stronger and filled with more want than he'd ever experienced.

Her fingers had locked in his short hair, pulling, holding him closer to her as her legs tightened around his hips.

His fingers shook as he unbuttoned her shirt, one small button at a time. His eyes soaked in the view of every exposed inch. When she lay below him, her shirt opened wide, his eyes roamed over her tan skin. She wore a silver bra, which cupped her perfect breasts, showcasing them only for him.

He ran a fingertip slowly down her neck, over her skin, as he watched her chest rise and fall with every breath.

When he looked, her blue eyes were watching him. Then she tilted her lips up and he noticed a sweet dimple at the corner of her mouth. Leaning down, he ran his mouth over the spot, wanting to capture the dip, explore it, memorize it forever.

His hands cupped her, causing her to throw back her head with a moan. He used this opportunity to bury his head in the crook of her neck, tasting and exploring every enjoyable soft curve.

He felt her hips moving against him and couldn't stop a matching groan from escaping his lips. His fingers shook slightly as he brushed them over the apex of her jeans.

She reached for his shirt and started pulling it over his head. She stopped with a gasp.

He glanced down and cussed under his breath. His bandage was covered in dried blood.

Instantly, she pushed away from him, trying to sit up. "I need to clean that."

He held her still by putting his hands on her shoulders. "Later." He almost didn't recognize his own voice. When she made a face, he chuckled. "Willa, I'm begging you." He pushed his hardness against her and watched her eyes go wider.

"Caleb, I…" He could see the hesitation in her eyes as they moved back down towards his bandage.

He sighed as he rolled off her and sat up on the end of the sofa. He kept his eyes closed as she moved around gathering the tools she would need to clean him up.

He opened his eyes again when her fingers brushed up against his ribs.

His hand snaked out and took her smaller one, holding it away from him. "You're trying to kill me, aren't you?"

Her eyes locked on his, and she shook her head. "I'm sorry; I didn't mean to hurt you."

He laughed, still holding her hands in his. "Not what I meant." He took them and covered his painful hardness.

She made a sexy growling sound, but then pulled her hand away. "First things first." Her eyes locked with his again.

Since he couldn't find his voice, he nodded instead. She bent her head and got to work cleaning his wounds. It was pure torture to have her fingers brush his skin as she worked. He wanted to be skin against skin, but the more she worked, the more he returned to reality.

After she'd covered his stitches with another white bandage, she leaned in and placed a kiss over his lips. He pulled back and took her shoulders with his hands.

"Willow, we need to talk." She leaned against him and frowned.

"You can tell me the rest of the story later." She started trailing kisses along his collarbone. She'd removed his shirt completely. Now he was sitting on her sofa, her skin pressed up against his and he knew he had to leave as quickly as possible. If not for her protection, for his own heart.

"I can't afford to be distracted right now." He watched her move away slightly. "Not to mention, it would be very bad if Al or Tony found me here, with you." He felt his blood turn hot at the thought of what they would do if they found out she was Billy's daughter. He pushed up from the sofa quickly and pulled back on his shirt. Then he walked over and picked up his jacket. "I'm sorry."

When he turned back towards her, he realized she hadn't moved. "I wish things were different." Her eyes avoided him and he could tell that the more he talked, the madder she was getting. So, instead of explaining, he walked over and grabbed the door handle.

"Caleb." Her voice stopped him. "Stay the night. It's late."

He glanced over his shoulder at her, his eyes heating at the sight of her standing a few feet away. Her hair was still messy from his hands running through it. Her lips called to him, making his desire jump to life again. But he knew he couldn't, shouldn't, get involved.

She quickly held up her hands. "You can have the sofa again." His eyes zeroed on the uncomfortable thing. "You checked out of your hotel. This way you can get a fresh start in the morning. I can even drive you to the bus station."

He thought about spending a night holed up somewhere waiting for the next bus to anywhere. He doubted they had been followed back to her apartment, so he figured there was no way the gang was going to find him here for one more night. Besides, he had to admit that he really didn't want to go. Not yet.

"Fine," he sighed. "I guess I could spend another night on that thing." He flipped the door lock and set his bag back down.

"Something tells me you know more about the journal, are you going to tell me what it means and why you have it?" Her question stopped him and he thought about heading out once more.

Willow waited. It was clear he was struggling with telling her everything. She still felt like she wasn't getting the entire story from him, but couldn't imagine why he was holding anything back.

Finally, after a moment of silence, he walked towards the sofa and sat down once more.

"This thing is uncomfortable as hell." He frowned and leaned back on the pillows.

Chuckling, she agreed. "It's the best I could afford at the moment."

"I thought you had a fancy job at the Gulfarium."

Her eyebrows shot up in surprise.

"How do you know where I work?" she asked, watching his face turn a light shade of pink. His eyes moved around and he nodded to her backpack.

"I noticed the Gulfarium patch on your emergency bag. Besides, I guessed that you had some medical training, after the way you stitched me up so well."

She could tell he was lying so she crossed her arms over her chest and waited.

"Fine, I told you I've been in town for a while. The first night, I went to your sister's work." She felt a spike of anger jump in her chest instantly, but he continued talking, his eyes zeroed in on her feet. "I watched her for a few hours, but knew that it would be impossible to approach her because of all the guys hanging around her. Then I saw you and followed you instead. I figured you'd lead me to Billy, but…" His eyes grew sad and she moved over to sit next to him.

"He really meant a lot to you?" she asked as she took his hand in hers.

His eyes moved back to hers and he nodded. "He's the only reason I'm alive. I can't tell you how much your father taught me in the short years I knew him."

Her throat had started closing up, so she swallowed hard and blinked a few times. "He was never really around long. Not that I can remember. Wendy remembers more of him than I do."

His hand reached out and he started rubbing her

shoulder. "I can only imagine what it was like. Always having him gone. But, know this, it wasn't his choice." He took a deep breath.

"How could it not be? He chose to leave each time." She leaned back as his hand dropped from her. She didn't want him touching her, not when he had gotten so much time with her father while she and Wendy had been left on their own.

"One of the first things I learned about the Lone Outlaws was that the higher members, like your dad, were so devoted, most of them gave up everything, including jobs, wives, and kids, to run the business. After your dad decided to start collecting evidence, he told me, the safety of you two became his number one priority. The more time he spent with you, the more chance the gang would have of finding out about you."

She felt her heart skip. "They didn't know already?"

He shook his head. "No one did. Your dad was a pretty private man. I only found out about you after we'd started talking to the cops."

"What does all of this mean?"

"All I know is that he always called it his insurance policy."

"For?"

He sighed and leaned his head back. "I'm not too sure on that myself. When your dad left, the last time"—his eyes locked with hers— "he told me to

87

hold onto it."

"Then why bring it back here? Why try and give it back to my father?"

"Because it's no longer safe with me." He was silent.

"Where are you going from here?" she asked after a minute or two.

"Does it matter?" His voice was low and she could tell he'd answered enough questions for the night.

"Well, if you're ever near here…" He sat up a little.

"What?" He almost laughed it. "Stop by and pretend to have a normal life?" Sarcasm rolled off every word.

"Why not?" She shook her head. "I mean; why can't you have a normal life?"

He leaned closer to her, running the back of his finger down to her chin. "Because for the past thirteen years, I've been under this great nation's protection as a witness, and now that several of the men I helped put away are running free in the streets, I doubt anything else in my life is going to be normal ever again."

Chapter Seven

*W*illow lay in her bed, staring at the ceiling fan, and felt like her eyes would never close. It wasn't as if she wasn't tired. Honestly, she was very tired, but Caleb's words kept playing over in her mind.

Witness protection. She'd never really thought it was a thing. I mean, sure, she assumed that it happened, but only in the past. She never really imagined that someone today could be in the program.

If her dad and Caleb had put everyone away for their crimes back then, why had he spent thirteen

89

years, most of his life hiding? From whom? Why? Didn't the cops know everything they needed to lock everyone up?

She was sure Caleb wasn't telling her everything. She could hear him in the next room, moving around, trying to get settled.

She'd never thought that her sofa was uncomfortable. Actually, when she'd bought the secondhand thing, she'd thought it was the softest one she tried out. But she was at least a foot shorter than he was, and she'd never actually tried to sleep a whole night on it either.

Finally, after almost a half an hour of hearing him wrestle with comfort, she opened her door and stood in the doorway.

Both of his feet were hanging off the end, his head was shoved into the corner, and half of his hip hung off the edge.

"Come on," she drawled. "No one ever said I was a bad host." She motioned towards her king-sized bed.

He sat up a little, his eyes going to the large bed. "Are you sure?"

She chuckled. "The bed is big enough for us each to take a side." She thought she noticed a slight frown on his lips, but he jumped up quickly and followed her back into her bedroom.

She thought having him next to her would settle some of the nerves in her, but instead, it just ignited even more.

Now, she could hear him breathing deeply next to her. Not to mention she could actually feel the heat radiating off his body from under the blankets.

"Caleb?" she said into the darkness.

"Hmm?" She felt him turn towards her, so she turned towards him.

"Why aren't you back under witness protection?"

She heard him sigh before he answered. "I was until Tony walked into the bar I was working at last month. By the time I called in to notify my contact, I was already on the run from them. So, I figured I'd hide out for a while, then swing by and drop this off to your dad before heading back in. Who knows where they were going to send me next."

She sat up a little. "But you said my father called you to Miami?"

He sat up a little, tucking his head under his elbow. He'd removed his shirt to sleep only in his boxers. Had she known that ahead of time, she would have never invited him into her bed. Or, maybe she would have.

"Yeah, he sounded like your old man, but something was off. So, when I reached out to my handler, I was told that they had been working on moving me anyway, since they had proof that my position was compromised."

91

"What does that mean?"

She felt him shift and guessed that he'd shrugged his shoulders lightly. "From what I can tell, after moving into Miami, it took less than two weeks for them to find me. I'm guessing the call was a setup to lure me somewhere they could get to me better."

"Why are they still after you?"

"Payback maybe. But, in the alley, before shooting at me, Al and Tony sounded like they were trying to recruit me again."

"Maybe they don't know you were the one to turn them in?"

He chuckled at that. "It would be hard for them not to since I sat across from them in the courtroom and confessed to everything I'd seen since becoming a member of the gang."

"Ohhh." She lay back down and crossed her arms over her chest. "What kind of things?" she asked after a moment.

"Willow?" His voice was softer.

"Hmm?" She felt her breath hitch. Instead of answering her, he rolled over until she was pinned under his hard body, his breath falling lightly over her.

"No more questions," he groaned just before his lips dipped to hers.

The kiss was different than before. Earlier it had been urgent. Now, however, his lips were feather light as he trailed his mouth over hers. His hands roamed slowly over her silk tank top and matching shorts.

Her fingernails dug into his bare shoulder blades, holding him closer to her as his mouth trailed down her jaw towards her neck. When he tugged her shirt over her head, she helped him remove the rest of their barriers until they lay skin to skin. Her legs wrapped around his hips, holding him closer. His fingers were gentle as he cupped and brushed over sensitive skin, following each movement slowly with his mouth and tongue until she was writhing underneath him, moaning and begging for something more.

"Caleb." Her voice sounded too far away. She was marveling in the taste and feel of him when he tugged her legs wider and settled his shoulders between them. His mouth covered her soft flesh as he lapped at her, causing her shoulders to bound off the mattress. Her fingers dug into his thick hair, holding him, guiding him to where she wanted, needed him most.

"My god," he croaked, then he was back up, covering her completely. "Tell me to stop," he demanded harshly.

Her mind and body were too heated; all she could do was shake her head from side to side. Then he was plunging into her, sending every one of her nerves shattering at the same time.

Caleb knew he was going to hell. If he doubted it, all he had to do now was open his eyes and look down at the goddess he'd just destroyed. Not that she looked like she'd done anything but thoroughly enjoyed his obliteration. But he knew there was no way now that he could ever leave her without losing part of himself. Not after what they'd just done. What they'd just gone through together.

"Don't leave tomorrow," she whispered next to his skin.

He didn't have the heart to answer her. Especially since there had been a heavy feeling pounding on his chest since the moment she'd invited him into her room.

"Sleep," he croaked as he turned and tucked her soft body next to his. His arms wrapped around her, holding her as close as he could. If he was going to be damned, he might as well enjoy the moment.

It took several hours for his mind to finally shut down. He'd listened to her soft breathing as she slept next to him. Finally, hours later, as the light streamed into the room, he felt her twist beside him.

"Morning." She smiled at him, her arms wrapping around his shoulders.

"Hey." He couldn't keep his eyes from seeking hers. "You okay?"

"Hmm." She smiled and leaned up to place a soft kiss on his lips. "Better than okay. You?" He watched her eyebrows squish up as she waited for his answer.

"I'm trying to convince myself that we didn't just make a big mistake." His fingers brushed down the side of her face.

"Why would this be a mistake?" He could feel her tense. He knew they had to talk about it sometime, but figured later was better. Especially since her soft body was pressed tightly against his and he was wanting even more of her.

"No reason," he lied, pulling her closer and leaning in for a kiss. By the time her lips parted, allowing him to swallow her moans, she had gone completely lax in his arms. Rolling, he tucked her underneath him again as her legs wrapped around his hips once more.

"Mmm, more," he begged, pushing her knee up to her chest. "I could spend an entire lifetime exploring your soft skin," he vowed next to her breast. "Running my mouth over every soft inch." He ran his tongue over the peak and lapped at the point and then took it into his mouth and sucked.

He heard her moan as she grabbed his hair, holding him, pulling him closer.

"Yes, Willa, just like that." His fingers brushed against her soft sex, parting her until he dipped into her heat and marveled at the fact that she was wet, waiting just for him.

He ran his thumb over the hidden nub as he sucked at her nipples slowly. He felt her hips start to move, grinding as she followed each movement from his fingers.

"Do you want me?" he asked against her skin.

To answer him, she pushed on his shoulder until he was sprawled back on her bed with her straddling him. Her hips and legs held him hostage as she leaned over him. Her long hair fell across his chest as her soft breasts brushed against his pecs.

He held onto the outsides of her thighs and begged her silently to straddle and ride him.

"The question is… how bad do you want me?" The slight smile on her lips caused his hips to jolt with need.

"Willa, you're playing with fire," he growled and squeezed his fingers on her thigh until she moved up and slowly slid down on him fully.

His eyes closed with the pure pleasure. His hips moved on their own, thrusting up until she followed his rhythm. When he opened his eyes again, she had leaned back a little, until her hair fell over those perfect breasts as her hips moved slowly over him. Her hands had bunched on his stomach, her nails digging into her soft palms.

She tossed her head back, closing her eyes as pleasure took her. He figured he could watch that show a million more times and never get bored of seeing her in complete ecstasy.

"More." This time it was a demand as he flipped her over, pushing her legs high up over his shoulders as he continued to pound into her soft flesh. Her eyes were glued on his, her mouth opened wide as he used her relentlessly. He could feel her building again as her nails dug into his arms. He watched her blue eyes go dark before sliding closed with pleasure.

Only when he leaned down and covered her lips with a soft kiss, did he finally allow himself to join her in complete satisfaction.

"Still think this is a mistake?" she asked a few minutes later as they stood in her small shower together.

He'd been admiring the colorful tattoo on her back. The happy sea turtles, dolphins, and fish swam towards her shoulders. He chuckled as he lathered her sexy body up with soap. "Most definitely." He turned her around and leaned down to place a soft kiss on her nose.

He couldn't stop the feeling that he was running headfirst down a path from which there would be no return. But something deep inside him demanded he continue. He needed this. Needed her.

He wanted the slight hints at an ordinary life with her. If he could live a somewhat normal existence in the next few hours, maybe he could be content with running for the rest of his life. Alone.

They sat around her small table and ate the breakfast they had cooked together. He'd teased her as they cooked, making sure to touch her as often as he could.

She walked around with a sexy white apron tucked over her old jeans and sweatshirt, looking sexier than if she'd been wearing silk and pearls. She'd braided her long hair to the side, only to have his fingers untangle the long locks.

He wanted to hold onto the magic spell that had trapped them both in the perfect world, but when her cell phone rang, their utopia was shattered.

"It's my sister," she said, frowning down at her phone.

He nodded as he leaned back in his chair. She walked into her bedroom to answer her sister's call and it felt like she'd just slammed the door on his dream life.

He carried their dishes to the sink, put on his boots, and zipped his bag. When she stepped out of the room less than five minutes later, she was chewing her bottom lip.

"Something wrong?" he asked as he pulled on his jacket.

"You're leaving?" she asked.

He frowned and looked down at his bag. "We both knew I had to." He couldn't look her in the eyes. Not since he knew exactly how she was feeling inside.

There was a moment of silence before she finally said, "I'll drive you to the bus station."

"No," he said quickly. "There's no need. Besides, I don't want to chance anyone seeing us together."

He heard her gasp lightly and knew what she was thinking. Rushing over to her, he took her shoulders with his hands and corrected himself. "Anyone being Al or Tony. They're still in town somewhere. Looking for me. I can't…" He shook his head. "I don't know what I would do if they found out about you… or your sister."

When he mentioned Wendy, Willow seemed to freeze with fear.

"Another good reason why I need to leave now." He leaned down and brushed her lips with his. "God…" The words tore from his lips. "I wish more than anything I could stay."

"Then do." Her arms felt so good wrapped around him.

Making up his mind, he tore himself free and walked to his bag without another word. When he opened the door, he glanced back and saw her standing there, her arms wrapped around herself as she cried silent tears.

He slipped from the room without another word and felt his heart shatter for the last time.

Chapter Eight

There was still too much to do and not enough time to accomplish it all. It was just over a month until Wendy and Cole's wedding and two weeks had passed since Caleb has walked out her front door.

She didn't know why, but she hadn't told anyone about Caleb's visit or her father's journal, which was still tucked deep inside her purse.

Since Willow was Wendy's maid of honor, she'd been running around every free moment in the last few days, helping her sister with last-minute details.

"You'd think you were hosting the Oscars,"

Willow complained.

Wendy laughed. "With as many news crews as I'm sure will be trying to sneak onto the beach that day, it will seem like it." Her sister frowned. "Maybe we shouldn't have the wedding on the public beach after all?"

Willow groaned. "You're not doing this again!" She put her hands on her hips and frowned at her sister. "Cole made me promise that I'd talk you out of changing the venue again."

Wendy sighed and then smiled. "Fine, but I'm going to look into adding more security."

"Aren't the Grayton guys going to be enough?" Willow joked.

Wendy laughed. "I love knowing that I'm marrying into a strong family."

Willow felt a pang of jealousy hit her mid-chest. Her sister must have guessed her pain, since she walked over to her and took her shoulders with her hands.

"Correction, we're marrying into a strong family."

"Yeah, right," she jeered under her breath.

"No, really. Besides, everyone already thinks of you as their younger sister." Wendy smiled. "Especially Shelly and Missy. If anyone has cause to know what it feels like as an outsider, they do."

Clearly trying to change the subject, Wendy

turned back towards the sales rack, searching for clothes she would wear on their honeymoon in Hawaii. "I mean; can you imagine hiding from your family for seven years?" Wendy sighed and glanced over at her. "It must have been hell living in fear for your life like Missy and Reagan had to."

Willow nodded, remembering how Missy and Reagan, her son with Roman, had hidden from her crazed father who was the head of a large cult. The man had been caught trying to kill her and her son and was now tucked away for life in some prison.

Then her thoughts turned to their own father, and she knew she couldn't hold her secret about him in much longer. But she planned on waiting until after their wedding.

"Here, what about this one?" Her sister's voice broke into her thoughts, distracting her once more from thinking about Caleb.

She'd figured out shortly after he'd left that she cared for him more than she ever had for anyone else. Her mind was constantly consumed with him. Worry dominated her thoughts. She wondered where he was, if he was okay. And if he was thinking about her and the night they had spent together.

Every time someone knocked at her apartment door, her heart would skip in hopes that it was him.

"I'm meeting Cole in half an hour at Cassey's. Why don't we head down and have a drink until he gets there?" Wendy's eyes lit up every time she mentioned her fiancé.

"Sure, I could use a drink after lugging around your packages all day." She smiled at her sister. Their relationship had changed for the better in the last six or seven months. Maybe it was because Wendy had stopped treating her like a child or it could be that Willow had done some growing up and actually started appreciating everything Wendy had done for her. After all, her big sister had played the role of mother and father for most of her life. She'd found out a few months ago that it had been Wendy paying her college bills instead of the scholarships, as she'd believed.

Her sister has done so much for her in her life, that there was no way she could ever repay her. But she planned on trying.

When they walked into the Boardwalk Bar and Grill, the place was packed. Alan and Steven were behind the bar, flirting with all the half-dressed ladies in their bikinis. Fruity drinks were pushed across the counter as loud music pumped out of the speakers. Families, couples, and large groups of people crowded around, waiting to be seating in the almost-packed dining area.

Willow really loved the place. Wendy had been lucky enough to get a job at the best place along the boardwalk. Not to mention that Cassey, her boss and best friend, was soon to be her new sister-in-law.

"There's Cassey." Wendy smiled and waved at

her friend, who was just coming down the back stairs. The woman glowed as she placed a hand on her growing belly. They had just found out three months ago that Cassey and Luke were having twins. Since then, Cassey had cut most of her workdays in half. She'd hired a floor manager to take over most of her work. Smiling over at her sister, Willow knew that Wendy had been the perfect choice for the job.

"I don't know how you bartend and help run this place." She sat on a bar stool next to Wendy, who just smiled at her.

"What can I say... I love my job." Her sister beamed.

There was no doubt in her mind that her sister did love her work.

"Not to mention, you're still finding time to plan your wedding." Willow leaned back and thought of all the things she had put on the back burner in the past few months.

Wendy set the bags down next to them and waved Alan over. "Alan, we need some drinks."

"You're usual?" he asked, moving around the bar as he worked quickly.

"Always," Wendy joked, turning back towards the door. "There's my man now. Right on time."

Willow watched her sister's face light up even more as she watched Cole walk towards them.

Every woman's eyes zeroed in on the sexy blond surf god as he walked across the room, but his eyes were locked on Wendy and his smile matched her sister's. When they came together, she heard several women sigh with jealousy, including herself.

"Hey," he finally said to her after they finished a quick sexy kiss. Cole's arm stayed around her sister's shoulders. "How was shopping?"

Wendy proceeded to talk about their day as he listened intently to every word.

Willow had never really felt jealous around the couple, until after she'd met Caleb. Now, every time she was around happy couples, all she could think about was him, and how lonely she was.

It had been hard the first few nights after he'd left. She'd lain awake in her bed, hoping, waiting for a sound at her front door. But each night she'd gone to bed lonelier than the night before.

She'd never felt this way about Jake. She ran the short time they'd been together over and over in her mind. The way he'd looked at her with his dark eyes and how his hands had felt running over her heated skin.

Every time she thought of him, her face flushed, and she realized she missed him more than she thought possible.

Even work held little interest for her the last few days. Often she found herself sitting in the sand thinking about him. Where he was. What he was doing. Was he safe? Had the gang found him? Was he thinking about her?

When she was working, she was scanning the beaches, looking for his familiar face or build. The white sands were slowly filling up with tan, muscular, half-naked men, and she didn't even give any of them a second look.

When she'd met Wendy earlier that day, her sister had asked immediately what was wrong. Willow had once again had to lie to her sister and tell her she wasn't feeling well.

"It's all that time you spend outside. It's not right. You're going to get sunburn and skin cancer," her sister had said.

"I wear sun block and cover myself. Besides, it's better than hiding in dark lights with a bunch of drunks around me," she teased back. "You live the life of a vampire and are marrying a sun god."

"Yes." Her sister's smile had grown. "Yes, I am." Thankfully, Wendy hadn't mentioned how she looked or acted any further that day.

Now, as they sat at the bar, drinking their drinks and munching on a plate of hummus and cheese sticks, she listened and watched as her sister and soon-to-be brother-in-law flirted with one another.

Again, she felt the stirs of loneliness creep into her mind. Even joking with Alan did little to lift her spirits.

She desperately wished Caleb had a cell phone or she knew where he'd been heading next.

After she was done with her drink and food, she excused herself. She hugged Wendy and kissed Cole on the cheek and walked out of the bar to let the couple continue flirting and smiling at one other. She walked along the boardwalk towards her car and thought about her life. The beaches were almost completely full at this time of the day. Families and couples walked or played in the crystal green waters and built sand castles in the white sand.

She loved spending a day at the beach, but even that didn't sound exciting anymore. Her job was the only thing she looked forward to anymore. She had the job she'd always dreamed of. Helping animals was something she'd felt strongly about ever since she was a child. Wendy had taken her to the beach one day and they had found a baby dolphin that had been beached. They had worked together to help drag the baby back out to the deeper surf and watched as it swam out to its mother. From that moment on, she knew what she wanted to do with her life. Even though she'd taken a few detours in high school, she had been destined to become a marine biologist.

She loved every part of her life, except for the loneliness. It was funny; she hadn't realized she'd been lonely until after Caleb left.

She was just unlocking her car when she heard a noise behind her. Glancing over, she frowned when the noticed that the darkened parking lot was empty. Her heart skipped a few beats as her eyes moved around. When she turned back to her car, she jumped when a hand reached out and held the door shut.

Her arms swung around and connected solidly with something, causing her to fall back against her car door.

"Easy," a familiar voice sounded close to her ear, causing her knees to melt.

"Caleb?" She half squealed, half moaned his name.

"Hey." His smile melted her knees the rest of the way and she gripped her car door just to remain upright. He was rubbing his jaw, where her fist had connected with it.

His hair had grown out and she loved the thick curls around his forehead. His dark eyes roamed over her quickly, making her entire body melt. He was wearing a black shirt with the same faded jeans from before.

"What are you doing back here?" The question was off her lips before she could stop it.

His smile faltered for a moment. Then his hands were on her shoulders, drawing her closer. "I'm afraid I need your help once more."

My god it was good to see her again. He hadn't

stopped thinking about her in the two weeks he'd been gone. Every night he'd lay awake in some dingy hotel room and think about her. Dream about her. Wanting her.

He felt the hairs on the back of his neck rise, so he grabbed her keys from her and walked her around to the passenger side of the car and helped her in.

When he got behind the wheel, he peeled out of the parking lot and kept glancing back in his mirrors.

"What's wrong?" Willow asked, turning around to look behind them.

"I ran into some trouble after leaving you." He watched as two lights followed him. He cursed under his breath and knew it was going to be a very long night.

"Are you okay?" Her hand reached out for his.

"So far, so good." He turned the opposite direction from her apartment and punched the gas pedal.

"Where are we going?" she asked, holding on to his arm.

"I'm sorry." He chanced a glance at her for a moment. "Somehow they found out about you."

Instantly, fear shot through her. "Wendy?" She reached in her bag for her phone.

"She should be safe enough. They don't seem to

know who you are, just that you helped me."

"How?" she asked, and he could see fear in her eyes.

He felt like a traitor but knew she deserved the truth.

"When I called my handler"—he waited until she nodded with understanding— "I told him about you. Not by name, but that I had a female friend in Surf Breeze. He asked for more info, but I only told him where you worked." He glanced at her once more. "You haven't been at work the last two days?"

She shook her head and he sighed with relief.

"I've taken a few days off to help Wendy shop for her wedding."

"Good." He rested back a little, until he spotted the same two lights behind them.

"How would telling someone from the FBI about me be dangerous?"

"I'm not sure. Maybe the guys on the payroll, but shortly after I made the call, I had a visitor."

"Are you okay?" Worry flashed behind her eyes again.

He nodded. "Yeah. At first I thought it was a fluke, but after switching cities and hotels, I called once more. This time, I gave him the wrong hotel and room number. I sat outside the other hotel until the same guy showed up."

"What did you do?"

"I came here as fast as I could." He'd been in an utter state of fear for her the entire trip, but he kept that information to himself.

"What do we do now?" she asked, glancing again behind them.

The headlights had disappeared, but that didn't remove the worry or the feeling that they were being followed.

"I'm not sure. All I know is, I don't think it's safe to go back to your place just yet."

"I should still call Wendy." She reached for her phone then leaned back as she held the phone to her chest. "What should I tell her?"

He thought about it for a moment. "Is she living with her fiancé?"

Willow shook her head no. "They decided not to live together until after the wedding."

"Tell her to stay with him until she hears from you again."

"What about… us?"

He sighed. "Do you have a friend? Somewhere out of town that you can tell her you're visiting?"

"Yes, I lived in Crystal Shores until just a few months ago, after the hurricane. I have a few friends living there still."

He nodded. "You can call into work, too. Tell

them you have to take a few more days off. Don't tell them anything else."

She nodded and then dialed. He heard her leave a message for what he assumed was her boss, David. After hanging up, she took a couple deep breaths as she looked down at her phone.

"What is it?" he asked as he pulled onto another back highway.

"I told myself I wouldn't lie to Wendy anymore."

"Anymore?" His curiosity peaked.

"Wendy and I... We haven't always been this close, remember?"

He nodded quickly, glancing once more in the rearview mirror. The lights were back, so he punched the gas once more.

"After she was hurt in the hurricane, I promised to be a better sister."

He reached over and took her hand. "By warning her, you are being a better sister."

She shook her head and for a moment, he thought she was going to cry. "I didn't tell her about you. About what you told me about our father."

He blinked a few times and understanding hit. "Why not?"

She shrugged and glanced out the window into the darkness. "I guess I didn't want her to worry. She's recently gotten a new position at the bar and grill and she's deep into planning her wedding."

He took up her hand and placed a soft kiss on her palm. "Tell her what you want, but I would be better if she stayed away from her place until she hears back from us."

She nodded then took a deep breath and dialed her phone.

Chapter Nine

$\mathcal{W}$illow waited, her heart jumping out of her chest with each ring. When she finally heard her sister's voice, her mind locked up.

"Hello? Willow? Did you butt-dial me?" She would have chuckled, except fear raced through her mind, images of her sister cut open, bleeding much like Caleb had been when she'd met him.

"Don't go home," she blurted out.

Wendy laughed. "Too late. What's up? You sound like someone from one of those slasher films you love." She heard Wendy laugh even more. She couldn't think of what to tell her sister, so she tried a different tactic.

"Is Cole there?" she begged.

"Yes, why?" She could hear the laughter die from her sister's voice.

"Let me talk to him," she said, biting her bottom lip and hoping her sister wouldn't ask why.

"Why?" Wendy asked, causing Willow to almost groan out loud. Willow could hear even more concern creep into her voice.

"It's a surprise," she lied and closed her eyes, praying her sister would fall for it.

"What?" Wendy asked.

"You know, for the wedding." She hated lying, but knew that Cole would be easier to talk to.

"Fine," her sister said after a moment. She heard the phone being passed off and felt a little relieved.

"Hey, Willow, what's up?" Cole sounded eager.

"Cole, I need you to step outside first," she begged.

"Okay." He drew out the word, but she could hear him walking outside of her sister's condo. "I'm out. Now what?"

"I need my sister to stay with you at your folk's place for a while." She knew she couldn't hide the worry in her voice and didn't even try with him.

"Why?" he asked slowly.

She took a deep breath. "It's a long story, but she might be in danger if she stays at her place."

"What?" Concern flooded his voice. "Are you okay?"

She nodded, feeling tears sting the back of her eyes. "It's about our father. The bike gang he was in… short story, they're looking for us. I'm safe. I'm staying at a friend's house in Crystal Shores until I hear more. I just need Wendy to stay with you, oh, and maybe you can make sure she's safe at work."

She glanced over and saw Caleb nod in agreement.

"Willow?" Cole's voice was low and she could hear the anger and concern.

"Please, just do this. It may be nothing, but I need to know that she's safe. Don't tell Wendy anything about this. Tell her something other than this. I don't want her worrying, not with everything she has on her plate. Besides, you know how she feels about our father. She might just walk into danger to spite his memory."

"Why—"

"I'll call you in a few days." She cut off his other questions. "Please, just do this for me."

The other side of the line was silent for a while. "Of course. But, text me where you're staying and let me know that you're okay."

117

"I will." She relaxed back. "Thanks."

"Sure. Now I'm going to have to make something up and lie to the love of my life." He groaned.

"Sorry." She felt guilt spreading but came up with an idea. "Tell her you're redecorating the place for her."

He chuckled. "It was going to be a surprise, but we weren't going to live here after the wedding. I bought a house down the street from Marcus and Shelly's."

"What?" She smiled. "Wow, congrats."

"Thanks." She could hear the pride in his voice. "I'll think of something. Be safe."

"I will. Take care of my sister," she begged.

"Always."

She held her phone and felt the tears sliding down her face. Wendy and Cole were so lucky to have found each other.

"Everything okay?" Caleb said, breaking into her thoughts.

"Yeah, Wendy's going to stay with Cole and his family at their place in Spring Haven. Across the bay."

"Good. Now we need to find a place for us." His eyes moved back to the mirror. "But first, we have to lose them." He nodded behind them. She turned around and saw two headlights.

"Who do you think is in the car?"

"Look again," he answered. "It's not a car."

She turned around in her seat so she could see. He was right; there were two motorcycles following them. They were spaced apart so that their headlights looked like a car instead of two bikes.

"How did they find us?"

He sighed and gripped the steering wheel tighter. "I should have known that they followed me from my last hotel. I bet they were just trying to get to you." He cursed under his breath.

"It's not your fault." Her eyes were glued to the lights behind them. "What do they want with me?"

He shook his head and reached for the glove box.

"What are you looking for?" She helped him open it.

"Everything with your name on it."

"Why?" She frowned.

"We need to get rid of it."

"Why?"

"Because at this point, they don't know you're Billy's kid," he burst out.

"So?" She wasn't following him.

He glanced at her. "If they found out... let's just say, I think it would be better if they thought you were just a friend of mine."

119

She thought about it, then started gathering up everything—her car registration, her license, her checkbook, everything. She never realized how much she had with her name on it.

"Now what?" she asked, holding everything in her lap.

"Toss it out the window." He nodded towards the side of her car.

"What?" she squealed.

"What else do you suggest we do with it?"

She thought of her credit cards, her license. How long it had taken her to apply for each one, what each one meant to her. She had about a hundred dollars on her in cash, but the rest of what she lived on was tucked safely into her bank account. And he was asking her to throw her entire identity out the window for anyone to find.

She thought about it. What else could she do with it all?

"Fine." She felt her heart sink.

"Toss them in a bag first. If they see you tossing out all that paperwork, they might stop to see what it is."

He kept his eyes on the road as she reached behind the seat and pulled the small black trash bag she used and tossed everything into it.

"Next turn I make, toss it hard so it clears the side of the road," he said, speeding the car up.

"I hope you have some cash, because I only have about a hundred."

He nodded without saying anything. She rolled down the window and waited. Her heart beat faster as the wind blew her hair around.

"Now," he called just after he turned off the highway. She tossed the bag hard, but hit her hand on the top of the door. She watched in horror as the bag bounced once on the side of the road, then rolled off into the grass. By the time the two lights hit the spot, the bag was out of sight.

She leaned back and rolled up her window.

"Did it clear the road?" he asked.

"Yes, I don't think they noticed it. Now what?"

"Now, we run faster than them."

Caleb drove for the next hour, thankful that the little car didn't need to be filled up every hour. Actually, he was pretty sure that the tank of gas in her car would outlast even the motorcycles following them.

The bikes were faster, but at this point, whoever was following them didn't seem to want to catch up, just follow.

Willow had become quiet next to him and when

he looked, her face was turned away from him.

They had talked for the first half hour. She had so many questions about where he'd been, what he'd been doing since he'd left her. Each question he had answered and he'd asked his own about what she'd been doing.

She kept telling him her life was boring, but so far he'd hung onto her every word.

"Are you okay?" he finally asked.

She looked over at him. "Yeah, I guess I'm just thinking about what to do next."

"Any ideas?"

"A few. You think that your contact, your handler, is in contact with the Lone Outlaws?"

"How else would they have been able to find me so quickly?"

She nodded and then was silent for a moment. "I had a thought on how to use that to our advantage."

"And?"

"Maybe we can mislead them again." She looked over her shoulder at the two lights that were still following them down the long back highways.

"To what end?"

"If we can lose them"—she tossed her head back towards the two lights— "then change directions, we can head back towards the coast. I might have a place we can hide out for a while without being noticed."

"And tell my contact what? We're up north?"

She nodded. "We've driven almost two hours this direction. Why would they believe we've circled back?"

He thought about his trick, the night in the alley, how he'd backtracked, knowing they wouldn't look for him where he'd just been. It had worked once; why wouldn't it work again?

"I'll have to do some fancy driving; you might want to hold on." They were quiet for a while as he scanned the roads ahead.

When the opportunity came, he jerked the wheel of the car to the side, turning off on a dirt road, then slammed on the brakes and shut down the lights. They sat in darkness until first one, then both bikes past them.

"How long should we wait?" she whispered. She didn't know why she felt the need to keep her voice down. It wasn't as if they could hear them, but she still felt the urge to keep her ears glued to every sound. The low rumble of the bikes had finally passed, and now only the sounds of crickets played outside the quiet car.

They waited for a while, and then he glanced back, throwing his arm over the back of her seat, and started to slowly back out. He made sure not to use his brakes when they rolled to a stop on the road. He switched gears on the car without coming to a full stop and punched the gas without turning on the lights.

"Sorry, we'll have to go slow until I feel we can turn the lights on." They crept along the dark road and she wished it had been a full moon that night instead of just the small sliver of light.

Over a mile later, he turned off on a side road and punched the gas after turning on the lights.

"This will lead us back to the main highway." He drove faster than he'd gone all night and she settled back in her seat and watched as small farms and open fields passed by them.

Every now and then she would glance over her shoulder. But, so far, there was nothing but darkness behind them.

Finally, they reached the spot where he'd turned off onto the back highway and he pulled over. "Do you think you can find that bag?"

She smiled and jumped out of the car as he turned so the headlights hit near the spot. It took her less than a minute for her to retrieve her belongings.

She tucked the back close to her and got back in. "Thank you."

He smiled. "I know what it's like to lose your identity."

They continued on the path towards her home, and only stopped once to fill up the small car.

"I take it back." He glanced over at her, her

eyebrows shooting up in question. "What I said about this car. I guess it does pay to have one that only needs to be filled up once every five hundred miles or so." She chuckled.

"So, where's this place you want to hide out at?" he finally asked.

She frowned as he pulled out of the gas station.

"You're not going to like it."

"Why?" He frowned, matching her face. "Is it an ex-boyfriend?"

She laughed sarcastically. "I wish it was that easy."

He shook his head, not understanding, but waiting patiently for her answer.

"No, it's my mother's place."

Chapter Ten

They drove in silence a little longer as she gave him directions. From what he could tell, the place was so far out of the way, they were sure to never be found by the gang.

"I didn't know your mother was still alive. I guess since you said Wendy had been the one to raise you... I just assumed."

She felt the pang in her chest that she always felt when she thought about her mother. "She's been dead to me for most of my life. She spent years in prison for drug and shoplifting charges."

"My mother spent some time in and out of jail too." He reached over and took her hand. "I guess neither of them would win mother-of-the-year awards."

She could tell he was trying to lift the mood, but the fact that she was about to see her mother again, after almost ten years, had her stomach rolling with disgust.

"Turn here." She pointed to the dirt road where her grandparents' farm had always been. They passed under the heavy wood sign that hung over the gated area. Rosburn Farms was etched deep in the thick oak.

She remembered seeing it last when she'd spent a few days' with her mother's parents when she was eleven. Wendy had wanted her to know the couple. Even though their daughter had turned out bad, Wendy thought they deserved a chance to know their granddaughter.

As her car bumped up the long dirt lane, she thought about her mother. Charity Rosburn, had been a wild child, born of hippy parents who were a lot older and didn't believe in punishing their child. Charity had grown up getting everything she'd ever wanted. She'd learned early in life about drinking, drugs, and sex. Her parents had run an organic farm just outside of Destin, Florida. They had made their money selling organic honey, eggs, milk, and other products to the tourist during the season.

Willow had heard that both of Charity's parents had passed away in the last seven years and she knew her mother was now running the farm with her new husband, Ralph.

"It looks like a pretty nice place," Caleb said, breaking into her thoughts.

"Looks can be deceiving," she murmured.

As they drove up, the lights flashed across the front porch. The place was dark except for a small gas fireplace on the wide porch. She could see two dark figures huddled together.

When the car stopped, another light flashed on the porch.

"Evening, are you lost?" a deep voice asked.

Willow opened her door and stepped out. She watched as her mother, the spitting image of herself twenty some years from now, stepped off the porch without a word.

She was wearing a long, flowing flowered skirt. Her short dark hair was sprinkled with an occasional silver strand and was tied back away from her face. Her mother's hands covered her heart as she walked closer to her.

"Willow?" her mother said before embracing her in a hug.

 Willow's entire body stiffened until she felt Caleb's hands resting on her shoulders.

"Evening, I'm Caleb Harris." He held out his

hand for the man to shake.

"Ralph. Why don't you two come on up and join us. We were just having some coffee and some of Charity's homemade apple pie."

Her mother had yet to say anything more to her. She was just holding onto her arm as tears streamed down her face.

She followed the men up to the porch and sat next to Caleb on a small sofa seat.

"What brings you two out our way?" Ralph asked, taking up his wife's hand.

"Well," Caleb said, glancing at her. "We were hoping to see if we can stick around for a while. We've run into quite a mess because of Billy."

"What's wrong?" her mother finally piped in, looking worried.

"It's nothing," she started to say, only to have Caleb take her hand.

"We'd like to just lay low for a while. You know, under the radar." He pulled her closer.

"It's because of the Lone Outlaws isn't it? Did they find out about you?" Worry flooded her mother's voice as she reached for her hands. Willow allowed her to take them, but held very stiff.

Willow waited, hoping Caleb would answer, but when he didn't, she nodded her head in agreement.

"You're welcome to stay as long as you need. There's plenty of room in the guest cabin," her mother said, shocking her.

When her mother had finally been released from prison, she'd moved back home. Her parents, spoiling her again, had quickly built a fifteen-hundred-square-foot cabin on the other side of the large barn that housed most of their animals.

"I can't ask—"

"You haven't," her mother interrupted her. "For over twenty years you haven't asked a thing from me. And for that same amount of time, I haven't done anything for you. Let me do this one thing now."

She looked into her mother's eyes. They were so much like her own, she found it hard to blink or breathe. She could tell she was silently begging, so Willow nodded her head and squeezed Caleb's hand tightly.

Caleb whistled as they walked through the front door of the "cabin." He'd never imagined staying in a place this grand. Nor had he imagined in any of his dreams that places like this existed.

"This is a cabin?" He turned and looked at Willow, who just stood inside the door, frowning.

"My grandparents built it shortly after my mother was released from prison," she said softly.

"What exactly did they do again?" he asked as he walked around the large two-story living area. There was a two-story stone fireplace on the back wall, with tall windows on either side.

There were two large sofas facing one another in the middle of the hardwood floor.

A gourmet kitchen sat on the other side of the room, filling up the back wall. A wood staircase went up to what he could tell was a loft bedroom below the vaulted ceilings.

"My grandparents started an organic farm. My mother runs it now."

"Organic?" He shook his head.

"As in, fresh eggs, meat where the animals haven't been shoved full of chemicals and antibiotics." The tone of her voice was sharp.

"Isn't that a good thing?" he asked, walking over to her. He could tell she was upset. When he put his hands on her shoulders, she tensed even more so he pulled her closer to him.

"Sure, yeah. I mean, it is for the animals and for the people eating them."

"Then what's the problem?"

She sighed and rested her head against his chest. "Nothing, it's just hard seeing her. Being here."

He ran his fingers through her hair and held her close. "You probably don't want to hear this, but you look a lot like your mother."

He felt her tense, and then she leaned back and looked up into his eyes.

"You're right. I didn't want to hear that."

He smiled, then placed a kiss on her lips.

"I've wanted to do that all evening." His hands ran up and down her back, holding her closer to him. He didn't want her to see that they shook, so he kept them busy running over her.

"I've missed you," she said as her fingers tugged on his hair, pulling him back to her lips.

It was like an explosion went off. All of a sudden, he couldn't get close enough to her. He couldn't stop wanting the taste of her or the feel of her next to him.

He backed her up until her legs hit the back of the sofa, then he bent her backwards until they rolled over it. She landed softly on his chest without breaking their kiss.

His fingers shook even more as he tugged her blouse open, exposing her soft skin covered only by a cream-colored bra.

When he tossed the shirt aside, she sat back, reaching for his shirt as her blue eyes ran over him. She was nibbling on her bottom lip, making him wish she'd hurry up and release him from the shirt. Finally, when she tossed it aside, she leaned back and gasped.

"What happened?" She ran her fingers over the

fresh bruises.

"I mentioned my run-in at my hotel." He sighed, remembering the blows he'd taken from Tony. "It's not as bad as the other guy got." He only fibbed a little as he tried to pull her back towards him, but she held firm.

"You need to put some ice on the bruises and some salve on the cuts." She started to get up, but he rolled with her until he had her pinned underneath him.

"What I need, right now, is you." He crushed his lips to hers. He took the kiss deeper and almost cried out in delight when he felt her legs wrap around his hips. She was pressed up against him and he worried that he'd built himself up too fast, not allowing for her to take her pleasure.

He tried to move back, but she held him prisoner with her legs wrapped around him. Her arms locked around his chest, pushing her softness against him.

"Willa, let me…" She broke in by dipping her tongue deep into his mouth, causing him to moan with pleasure.

"Now," she begged when she finally backed away. "Please, Caleb."

Looking into her eyes, he realized he would never be able to deny her anything. Ever.

The rest of their clothes hit the floor quickly. She chuckled nervously as he tucked her jeans off her hips, taking her silk panties along with them. When he dipped his head down and swiped his tongue over her softness, she arched with pleasure, tugging on his hair, holding him, directing him where she wanted.

He couldn't get enough of her. She was the richest honey he'd ever tasted. He dipped his fingers and tongue into her until he felt her legs shiver around him. Then, and only then, he climbed back up until he could look her into her beautiful eyes as he claimed her once more.

Her soft moans undid the last hold he had on his restraint. His fingers dug into her soft skin as he took her, trying to hold her closer, longer.

He rained kisses down her neck as her hips moved with him. Her soft voice begged him, urged him to move faster, harder, and deeper. He obliged and felt a sense of pride when he felt her convulse around him. But he wasn't done with her yet.

Moving quickly, he gently picked her up in his arms and started up the stairs in hopes that the bed would be big enough. When he reached the top, he smiled and walked towards the king-sized canopy bed that sat in the middle of the loft area.

"I'm beginning to like your mother's tastes." He chuckled as he laid her down on the mattress and smiled when he noticed the mirrored ceilings of the canopy bed. "Really enjoying her tastes."

Willow chuckled a little and pulled him down over her. "I've never done this while watching before." Her eyes were glued to the mirrors.

"That makes two of us." He rolled a little so they lay sideways, both of their eyes glued to the image above. "I guess we'll have to experiment to get it just right." He watched his hand run over her soft skin in the image above.

When her eyes grew wide with pleasure, he moved behind her and then slid slowly into her as they watched every move.

Her hips arched back towards him as he ran his hand up to cup her perfect breast. Their eyes locked above and he watched her tongue dart out and lick her bottom lip.

"I've dreamed of you." It came out as a whisper next to her ear. "Of doing this to you." He jerked his hips and watched her eyes slide close.

"Me too," she moaned, her fingers going over his as they covered her chest. They locked fingers with one hand as his other crept up to play with her soft skin.

Her skin glowed with pleasure as he took his time running his hands over her, enjoying the view and the feeling of her next to him.

"I'm never sleeping in a simple bed again," he said against her skin. Hearing her giggle sent waves of desire through him, which caused his movements to speed up. Within moments, they were both gasping for breath, holding onto one another as they cried out in unison.

Chapter Eleven

When the sunlight broke in behind Willow's eyelids, she tried to roll over and cover her face, but bumped into a solid mass instead. Cracking open her eyes, she smiled up at Caleb as he lay, looking down at her.

"You're beautiful when you sleep." He brushed a strand of her hair away from her face.

"My sister always told me I snore," she joked.

"Not loudly," he teased. "Have you seen the bathroom in this place?"

She shook her head and thought about escaping

137

to the room and finding a tube of toothpaste and, if she was lucky enough, an extra toothbrush.

"The shower is incredible." He sat up and tugged her with him.

"Is it mirrored?" she joked, only to have his eyebrows wiggle up and down as he nodded. "You're kidding."

"Nope, two walls of reflective glass. This could get dangerous." She followed him into the bathroom.

The bathroom and shower were just as she imagined. Grandiose bordering on gaudy. All in all, though, she had to admit, the shower did wonders for making her feel loose. Of course, it was more about what Caleb had done to her, and she had enjoyed watching their steamy reflections.

When they walked downstairs, dressed in the same clothes from the night before, there was a light knock on the front door.

Caleb looked out the glass and then opened the door to Charity. It still shocked Willow to see how much the two of them looked alike. Her mother's hair was a lot shorter, though, cut to just below her ears, which highlighted the natural waves even more.

"I brought you some fresh eggs and milk. We'll run to the grocery store today to get anything you two might need." She walked in, looking relaxed and at home in the place. Of course, she had lived here for over ten years, until her parent's death, six months apart from each other. Willow had heard that her grandmother had died of breast cancer, while her grandfather had died a couple months after of a broken heart.

"Thank you, we can make a list for you." He walked into the kitchen and helped her with the items.

"I hope you'll feel free to make yourselves at home here." Her mother's eyes locked with hers. Willow's back stiffened as she nodded instead of replying. "There's some of my old clothes still up in the closet that should fit you. I'm afraid I don't have any..."

"I've got my own. Willow didn't have time to pack anything."

"I understand. Help yourself to whatever you find." It was silent for a moment while she watched her mother grip her hands nervously. Willow did the same movement occasionally; she hated that she was anything like the woman standing before her.

"How's your sister? I hear she's getting married?" her mother asked.

Just the mention of Wendy had Willow turning away from the woman, towards the fireplace.

"Well, if you need anything else..." She heard her say to Caleb, who walked her to the door.

"Hey." His voice was right beside her and when his hands fell on her shoulders, she relaxed. "Talk to me."

She turned and wrapped her arms around him. "Because of her, Wendy was never given the opportunity to be a real teenager. Because of that woman, I was teased for having a mother who was a crackhead and a thief." She realized tears were rolling down her face, soaking Caleb's shirt.

"Have you taken a good look at the woman?" he asked, pulling back. His hands were on her shoulders, holding her still as he looked deep into her eyes. "I mean, really looked at her. I can't say anything about her past, but it seems to me that the woman has not only cleaned up but moved on with her life."

She blinked a few times. "I'm not saying—"

"No, don't defend your feelings. I'm not against you." She had been about to defend herself. She'd acted the same way every time Wendy asked her to try to have a relationship with Charity. Her sister had been trying for the past five years to get her to visit her mother. She kept telling her how Charity had changed. How much she wanted to be a part of her life now. But Willow would never listen to her. Not with all of the hate and hurt built up from the past.

"From the sound of it, Wendy's feelings for your father are the same as your feelings for your mother."

She thought about it and nodded slightly.

"Well, you keep trying to persuade her about your dad. Maybe you also need to have an open mind about your mother."

It was like being stabbed in the chest. Something shifted when the simple truth was put in front of her.

She had been closed-minded as far as Charity goes. For years, she'd begged Wendy to love their father, but Wendy had always thought of Billy as nothing but a deadbeat father. Just the way she thought of Charity.

She closed her eyes. Her mother had changed since the last time she'd seen her almost ten years ago. The woman that was just here was nothing like the skinny drug addict who'd been shaking so badly, Willow hadn't even wanted to touch her.

"I'll think about it. What would you do if it was your mother, trying to act like nothing had happened in the past. That she hadn't abandoned you to the streets?" It came out as a whisper.

She could tell he thought about it for a moment before answering. Then he wrapped his arms around her and spoke into her hair. "I guess I'd listen to what she had to say before I made any judgements."

She took a deep breath, inhaling his wonderful musky scent before nodding her head slowly. "I guess I should at least listen to what she has to say first."

"Good. Now that that's settled, how about I make us some scrambled eggs?"

She felt her stomach growl. "Sounds good."

They spent the rest of the day trying to plan out their next step. Since he wanted to stake out the property and look for any weak spots that might pose a security threat, he suggested they take a long walk around the land.

Willow had jumped at the chance to get outside, since they had spent several hours stuck in the car last night.

"I guess I'm spoiled since I'm used to working outdoors now." Her hand felt good tucked into his own as they walked. She was still wearing her own clothes, and he wondered if she'd take her mother up on the offer of using some of hers.

"It must be nice. Doing what you always dreamed of." He held onto her arm as they jumped across a small stream of water.

"Yes and no. I mean, I always thought that life would challenge me a little more."

He laughed at her naivety. "You're not done living yet. I'm sure there are plenty of challenges still waiting around the bend."

She smiled up at him. "I mean; I hadn't expected to land my dream job the first place I applied."

"Maybe it was fate?"

"Maybe…" She seemed to be deep in thought. "I

often wondered if my mother had anything to do with my job."

"What do you mean? How would she have anything to do with getting you a job at the Gulfarium?"

She walked over to a tall wood fence and propped one of her feet up on the bottom rung. He stood next to her, leaning back on the fence as he watched her gaze out at the field that housed several dozen cattle, which were grazing peacefully.

"Her family has a lot of influence around here. My grandfather was on the county board of directors for years. There was a group of good-old boys that used to run everything in the county. When he died, well, let's just say my mother would have gladly used those influences for her own gain."

"You're thinking of the past again. Projecting what you knew about her back then to now."

She shook her head and looked up at him. "No, back then, my mother was a selfish child. Someone who wanted to experiment without paying consequences."

"And now?" He brushed a strand of her honey-colored hair away from her face.

"In the last few years, she's gained a reputation as a woman who's not afraid to use her family's power. A few years ago, the county tried to ban the sale of raw milk. I didn't witness it myself, but I heard that at a particular board meeting, she showed up at didn't end well. Needless to say, the new bill was dropped and she continues to be one of the biggest distributors of raw milk around."

"That doesn't necessarily mean that she would use her power—"

"Caleb, I'm not trying to accuse her of anything, but since I started working at the Gulfarium, I've heard her name dropped a few times here and there."

He nodded. "Still, shouldn't you be thanking her?"

Willow sighed and glanced off towards the field again. When a slight smile played on her lips, he knew she'd rationalized everything.

"I suppose you're right. I guess I'll never know until I actually ask her."

He brushed his hand down her back and pulled her closer. "From what I can see around here, she works hard for everything she has. It can't be easy running this place. Or fighting against powerful men who want to stop her from doing business. It takes a lot of guts to change your life around. Trust me, I went from selling drugs on the streets of Vegas to turning informant and putting away some of the biggest drug dealers in the States."

"I don't know how you did it." She wrapped her arms around his shoulders.

"I couldn't have, if it wasn't for your dad." She felt so good in his arms, he could easily stay where they were for the remainder of the day.

"I'm happy he helped. I still don't know how I'm going to tell Wendy about him. About you."

He couldn't stop the sigh from escaping his lips. "Maybe you won't have to." He held her close and thought about their next move. He'd given up years ago dreaming of having a normal future with someone. After all, he didn't know who else was out there, looking for him, looking for revenge. They had mentioned wanting to take him back, but he knew he'd rather die than to step foot in the lion's den that was the Lone Outlaws' home base.

"I'm going to head into town tomorrow." He felt her stiffen, so he rubbed her shoulders. "Just to make a quick call. I want to make sure they won't be able to trace the call, so I'm going to buy a disposable phone."

She looked up at him and nodded. "I'll go with you."

He quickly shook his head. "No, I want you safe and sound here."

She reached up and took his face in her hands. "If you think I'm going to sit around this farm while—"

"Willa, please. I don't know what I'd do if I put you in danger again. Besides, maybe you can spend the time with your mother?"

He saw the determined look in her eyes and knew that he'd have to outmaneuver her if he planned on getting her to do what he wanted.

"We'll talk about it later. Why don't we head back in and see if your stepdad is back from the store with our supplies?"

"Don't call him that." She frowned, her bottom lip going out slightly. He wanted to lean down and place a kiss on the pucker, but she backed up a step and crossed her arms over her chest. "That man is nothing to me, let alone any kind of dad."

He nodded. "Fair enough. Let's see if Ralph is back from the store with our supplies." He smiled when she nodded her head quickly. He wrapped his arm around her as they walked. "You okay?" he asked after a moment of silence.

"I guess I'm just moody. I can't believe I'm actually here." She looked around again and let out a deep breath. "There were so many times I'd dreamed about living here, instead of in the small apartment with Wendy." She stopped quickly. "Not that I didn't want Wendy to come with me, it's just... I'd always hoped that my mother would change and come and get me, come get us. So we could live here, with all the animals. Not to mention having actual adults in the house watching over us."

"I suppose neither of us knows what that's like."

"I've often wondered..." She bit her bottom lip, her blue eyes searching his. "Never mind."

"Oh no," he joked. "Don't hold back. Tell me." He took her hips in his hands and pulled her back towards him.

"It's nothing." She waited and when he continued to hold her close, she sighed and finished. "I've often wondered if I would end up being a terrible mother, like she was."

It cut him straight to his heart. Hadn't he thought the same thing? He used to fool himself that he'd never allow anyone to get close to him, since he was surely as damaged as his mother had been. Who, in their right mind, would ever want to be with someone who, at the drop of a hat, could be so self-centered?

"I've thought the same thing about myself." It came out as a whisper. "But I'd like to think that we make our own fates. Just because we didn't have great role models doesn't mean that the know-how isn't locked somewhere deep inside us." He tapped her chest lightly, then his own. "I think you'd make a wonderful mother." He leaned down and placed a kiss softly on her lips.

"You're not pregnant?" He heard her mother's voice from a few feet away. They'd been so caught up in their conversation, that they hadn't heard Charity and Ralph approach them on two large black and brown horses.

Willow laughed and took a step back. "Of course not." It came bursting out of her.

The air was still for a moment and everyone silently looked at one another before Ralph jumped in.

"I've stocked your fridge and cupboards. You should be set for a while, but if you need anything else, give me a shout."

"Thanks." Caleb nodded and took up Willow's hand since she was fidgeting with her jacket zipper.

"I didn't know you had horses." Willow slowly approached them.

"Ralph persuaded me to get a few horses last year. They help when we want to check up on the cattle. If you want, feel free to take them out. They are both so gentle." Her mother leaned down and pet the mane of the horse she was on. "Maybe you'd like to go riding with me tomorrow?"

Willow looked towards Caleb and he gave an encouraging nod of his head.

"I'd like that." He could hear the hint of unsureness in her voice.

"Let's say around noon?" Her mother's voice was full of excitement.

Willow nodded her head in agreement.

"Perfect, I'll meet you in the barn at noon." Her mother's smile doubled.

"Well, we'd better let you two get back to your walk," Ralph said, tipping the straw hat that was on his head. "Evening."

"Night," Caleb said, taking up Willow's hand and heading back towards the cabin. They walked in silence for a while until they reached the back porch of the cabin.

"I'm not sure I should go." She sat in the large glider. He followed her, taking her hand in his.

"Why not? I thought you'd made up your mind to give her a second chance?"

She nodded slowly. "I have." She took a couple deep breaths. "But that doesn't mean it will be easy."

He chuckled and pulled her closer. "Nothing in life worth obtaining ever is." He placed a soft kiss on the top of her head as they watched the sun sink below the trees.

Chapter Twelve

Willow was more nervous than she'd been on her first date in junior high. Her palms were sweaty and she was finding it hard to hold onto the reins. Her pulse kicked every time she thought about opening her mouth.

She knew she had to say something, but every time she thought of something, she felt her jaw freeze up. So many questions popped into her mind.

She didn't want to listen to excuses of why her mother hadn't been there. Why she hadn't cared enough to stop her reckless life and take care of her responsibilities.

"I'm so happy you decided to come here." Her

mother broke into her thoughts.

Willow looked over and saw that there were tears rolling down her mother's face. Just the sight of them caused her heart to melt a little.

"I didn't know where else to go," she said truthfully.

"What about Wendy?"

"She's staying with her fiancé, Cole."

Her mother nodded and used the sleeve of her jacket to wipe the tears from her face.

"You don't have to cry, you know." It came out a little harsh, so she followed it up with. "Caleb won't let anything happen to us."

"It's not that." Her mother pulled on her reins until the horse stopped. Willow did the same and stopped right next to her. "I've spent years wondering how to mend this." She motioned between them. "I was young and stupid when I fell in love with your father. Billy was…" She sighed. "Everything I'd ever dreamed of. He was tall, handsome, charming, and a big enough bad boy that it would piss off my parents." She chuckled softly. "I was spoiled and selfish."

Willow watched her mother's fingers fidget with the horse reins, then glanced down at her own fingers and realized she was doing the same thing and stopped.

"I wish there was a magic time machine to take me back and give me—us—a second chance."

More tears rolled down her mother's cheeks. "I would do anything, give up anything, to have a second chance with you."

Willow's throat closed up and she felt her own tears sting the back of her eyes.

"I won't ask for forgiveness because, let's face it, I don't deserve it, but I will ask for another chance at being friends. I know you don't want or need a mother at this point, but maybe you could use a friend?"

It took a moment for her to answer, and when she did, her voice cracked and wavered. "I'd like that." She had to sniffle and wipe her own tears on the sleeve of her light jacket.

Her mother smiled and did the same with her jacket. "Now, let me show you the rest of the farm."

They spent the next hour riding the fence line of the field. When they came upon a calf that had gotten stuck in the fence, Willow helped her mother pull the small thing free of the wires and put salve on the few cuts in his back hide.

"Why didn't you sell this place? You know, after your parents... Grandma and Grandpa died?"

Her mother smiled as she mounted her horse again. "I guess you could say spending years behind bars changed me. After being locked up for so long, all I could dream about was being back here." She sighed and looked around. "I never would have imagined that this place could mean so much to me."

"Do you love it?" She didn't know what had caused her to ask the question, since she could already see it in her mother's eyes.

"More than I ever dreamed I could. What about you? Do you love your job at the Gulfarium?"

Willow nodded her head slowly. "Did you have anything to do with me getting the job?"

Her mother was silent for a while. "No, not me directly."

"Who then?"

"Ralph." Her mother started walking her horse again. Willow jumped up on hers and followed.

"Ralph? What do you mean?"

Charity glanced over at her. "Ralph owns the place."

"What?" Willow almost fell off the back of the horse as her mother chuckled.

"I mentioned to him that you'd just graduated from FSU and how worried I was that there weren't enough jobs out there to support a young woman such as yourself."

"Ralph owns the Gulfarium?" She couldn't seem to wrap her mind around it.

"Yes, and several other animal habitats along the coast. The Dolphin Preserve in Panama City Beach, several local no-kill animal shelters, and a few other businesses."

"Ralph?" Willow glanced back up towards the house. Ralph was tall, thin, and somewhat good-looking, but she would have never pegged him for a business owner. Especially one of so many large and successful businesses.

Ralph's silver hair and short beard made him look years older than her mother, but now that she thought about it, she supposed that they were almost the same age. "I guess I owe him a thank you." She turned to her mother. Her words stuck in her throat when she saw the amount of pleasure in her eyes. "How did you two meet?" Willow asked as they started to make their way back towards the barn.

"That's a funny story." Her mother proceeded to tell her how she'd met Ralph when she'd run over a small raccoon. She'd taken the hurt animal to the local clinic. Ralph had been working behind the counter and she'd assumed that he was just an employee. He'd taken the hurt animal to the back and proceeded to work on it himself.

"So, naturally, I then assumed that he was the veterinarian." She chuckled as she started to brush the horse down. They had made it back to the barn and had removed both horses' saddles. They took turns brushing the animals down and feeding them hay and grains. "Well, when he came out and told me that the poor creature hadn't made it, naturally I was upset. So you can imagine my surprise when he blurted out a dinner invitation."

Willow smiled. "So you went out with him then?"

"No." Her mother smiled and leaned back against the horse's neck. "I was upset that he would even ask me after telling me he couldn't save the raccoon."

Willow frowns. "What happened then?"

"I told him where to go." Her mother laughed. "And stormed out."

"But?"

"Then, after I'd cooled off for a few days, I had a knock on the door and imagine my surprise when it was Ralph standing there with a small box. I was instantly worried that he was stalking me, but he told me he'd gotten my address off the information I'd filled in at the clinic. He then showed me a box full of baby raccoons that needed help. It turns out that he'd gone to check out where I'd hit the poor thing and found the babies not far away."

"What did you do?"

"Well, I took them in of course, and went out on a date with Ralph. Any man who would go out in a rainstorm and find four helpless baby raccoons and nurse them back to health was okay in my books."

Willow chuckled. "What happened to the raccoons?"

"Oh, they're around here somewhere. When they got big enough, we turned them loose. They come up to the main house every now and then, begging for some of my pecan pie."

They were silent as they finished up in the barn. As they walked back towards the main house, her mother turned to her. "Would you two care to join us for dinner tonight? Ralph put a brisket on earlier today. I'm sure there's plenty for all of us."

"Well..." She thought about Caleb's words, about giving her mother another chance. Hadn't she listened to everything the woman said today with an open mind? Why then did she still hesitate when asked if she wanted to spend more time with her and the man who was responsible for giving her the dream job?

"Sure, I'll just want to clean up first." She looked down at her dirty jeans and shirt.

"How about we say in an hour?"

Willow nodded and turned to go.

"Willow?" her mother called after her. She turned back towards her. "I'm glad you went on that ride with me today."

Her mother held her breath for a response.

Willow smiled. "Me too." And she meant it.

Caleb was pacing the floor downstairs, waiting for Willow to finish getting dressed after her shower. He'd changed into a pair of dress jeans and a button-up shirt.

The talk he'd had with Ralph that morning while the ladies had been on their ride had opened his eyes a little more about the man.

"So…" Ralph slapped him on the back as he helped the man clean out the stalls in the barn. "You've got it bad, huh?"

"Is that really what you wanted to chat about while shoveling shit?"

The man had burst out in laughter. "No, that's just an observation." They cleaned for a while longer, and when they were laying the fresh hay down, Ralph turned to him and said. "Just how bad of trouble are you two in, son?"

Caleb set down the pitchfork and leaned against it. "Pretty bad. I think I've really screwed things up. Not only with my life, but now I've dragged Willow and possibly her sister into things as well."

Ralph tilted his head and looked at him. "Billy really did a number?"

Caleb shook his head. "It's not all Billy's fault. Not really. I made a promise to him to never go looking for him or the girls."

"Why did you?"

Caleb shrugged his shoulders and looked out the barn door towards the field where he knew Willow was out riding horses with her mother.

"I guess I just wanted to see if it was true."

"What?"

"That he could really stay hidden for all those years without thinking about me." He tossed down the pitchfork and shoved his hands into his pockets. "I mean; he was like a father to me. Then he just up and left me in the hands of the government while he ran back to his happy life."

He didn't know where the bitterness had come in, but something shifted in his chest just getting it out in the open.

Ralph walked over to him and put his hand on his shoulder. "Son, I never knew the guy personally, but from what I hear, both Charity and he were pretty screwed up back then. We all make choices, mistakes, when we're younger." The man exhaled and glanced out the doors. "From the sound of it, you've made a few yourself. What separates us from apes is the ability to learn and grow." He nodded off towards the cabin. "I've just met Willow, but since she's so much like her mother, I can see the look in her eyes when she looks at you. Don't make another mistake as you find a way out of this mess."

Caleb bobbed his head and bent to pick up the pitchfork again.

Over the next half an hour, Caleb had found out a little more about the man. Charity was his first wife and he had no kids of his own. He'd had a high school sweetheart, but she'd died at a very young age and he'd spent most of his young life mourning her.

Ralph made himself very clear that he meant business when it came to keeping Charity and Willow safe.

He was shocked to find out who the man was and the businesses he owned. He could see where his personal loyalties could easily translate to the business world and his love of animals.

After helping out in the barn, he followed the man out into the greenhouse and helped him with all of the plants. He'd never been around growing things before and found the chores absolutely fascinating.

He'd even started dreaming about a little garden of his own, with Willow. Close to sunset, he started back towards the cabin to shower and change for dinner. Ralph had invited them up to the main house that evening.

"Well?" He heard her soft voice from the top of the stairs. When he looked up, he lost his breath completely.

She was wearing a simple black spaghetti-strapped dress. Her long hair was tied up in a bun at the top of her head with curly whisks falling around her face. When she came down the stairs, he noticed the thin heels she was wearing and he felt his mouth go dry.

As she stopped in front of him, his arms wrapped

160

around her waist automatically.

"You look amazing." He thought he heard his voice crack, so he quickly leaned in and placed his lips over hers before she could laugh at him.

"Thank you, so do you." She smiled up at him after he'd pulled away.

"Are you sure we have to head over for dinner? I'm pretty sure what I want to enjoy is right here." His fingers dug into her soft hips, pulling her closer.

She laughed and tried to pull back. "I'm trying to make an effort with my mother, remember?"

He loved seeing her smile and hearing her laugh. Seeing her happy was almost as good as seeing her laid out below him as he took her.

Taking her hand, he pulled it up to his lips and placed a soft kiss on her knuckles. "Then we'd better get going. We're already past our hour mark."

Caleb had never sat down for a family meal before, either with his family or that of a girl he was interested in. He was nervous and unsure of how to act. Thankfully, he was saved any embarrassment the moment they got there when Ralph answered the front door in a shirt covered in mashed potatoes.

"Sorry, there was an... incident in the kitchen." He chuckled. "Make yourselves at home. Charity is in the kitchen cleaning up. I'll just run upstairs and change out of this." He motioned towards his ruined shirt.

161

"It's still so hard to believe that he's my boss," Willow whispered. "Well, not my boss, but my boss's boss." She shook her head as she walked further into the living room. "I remember coming here twice when I was a kid." She crossed her arms over her chest and walked towards the fireplace. "The first time was with my mother, before..." She turned and looked at him, so he nodded his head in understanding. "Anyway, she got in an argument with her father, my grandfather, about something while I played with an old dog they had." She stopped and looked down at the rug that sat right in front of the hearth. "The second time, Wendy had forced me to try and be nice with my grandparents after my mother was locked up. They were old and smelled like ham," she blurted out.

He chuckled as he walked closer to her. "I don't even know if my grandparents are still alive." He wrapped his arms around her waist.

"What about your mother?" Willow frowned up at him.

He only had time to shrug before Willow's mother came rushing in. Her hair was slightly messed up and there was a hint of mashed potatoes on her blouse.

"Sorry, the blender decided to blow up." She was smiling as she walked in and gave Willow a slight hug. "Would you two like something to drink? We have sweet tea or coffee?"

"Tea is fine," he said, noticing how Willow had

tensed slightly when her mother had gone in for the hug.

"I can help." Willow started to move towards the kitchen.

"Oh, nonsense. You're our guest tonight. We don't get too many people visiting out here, so you'll have to pardon us as we try to spoil you."

Her mother disappeared back into the kitchen and returned in a few minutes with a tray of glasses and a pitcher of tea.

"Sit." She motioned towards the sofa. He took Willow's hand and moved closer to sit down.

"I hope you didn't go through too much trouble for us," he said, tucking Willow close beside him.

"No trouble at all," Charity said, setting the tray down and pouring them each a glass of tea. "Ralph likes to cook. Actually, we both do. Besides, this way you can taste firsthand what we do around here. He started smoking the brisket early this morning. The meat is from one of our own cows and all the vegetables we pulled directly from our greenhouse. I had it built shortly after my parents passed."

She took a sip of her tea just as Ralph came rushing back down the stairs. "Sorry about that." He moved to sit down next to his wife, putting an arm around her shoulder as she leaned closer to him. "How was your ride?" he asked Willow.

Willow started talking about helping the calf that was stuck in the fence. As Caleb listened to her story, he looked at Ralph and Willow's mother. The couple looked completely content together. It was a little disturbing to see how much Willow looked like her mother. Actually, if he hadn't known any better, he would have assumed that they were sisters instead of mother and daughter.

He'd been impressed with Ralph after just a few minutes of talking to him earlier that day. The man seemed to know how to take care of himself and the people he loved. They had come up with a short-term plan to protect Willow when he had to leave her side.

He knew that when the time came, he'd get arguments from Willow, and he'd talked to Ralph about those concerns. Ralph had been very adamant about not keeping her in the dark about his intentions. He knew there was no way, when it came time for him to hit the road again, that she would want to be dragged around. She deserved a better life than always looking over her shoulder.

She'd talked about kids earlier, and he knew that even though she'd stressed her concerns for turning out like her mother, she still dreamed of having a family someday. And families meant normal lives.

Ralph had been very interested in finding out more about his contacts and handler information. He'd given him Agent Minster's information and told him about the last two times he'd stopped and stayed, how Al and Tony had shown up shortly after his first call and how the last guy, someone he didn't recognize, had found him the time after that.

They had actually come up with a slightly different plan than Willow and he had earlier. He glanced over at Willow and realized he hadn't had a chance to tell her about it yet.

"So, Caleb and I were talking earlier about your predicament." Ralph leaned in and took a sip of his tea.

"Maybe we can chat about it over food; everything should be just about done," Charity broke in. "I'm sure everyone's ready to eat."

They all moved into a large dining room, where the table was made up to look like a fancy restaurant. He'd never gotten the chance to eat anywhere expensive. He'd worked as a bus boy at a steak house once in California, but he'd been fired for dropping too many plates.

To say that he was impressed with the meal would have been an understatement. First, they brought out a fresh spinach salad with homemade raspberry dressing. There was freshly baked bread that steamed when broken open. Charity passed him a butter dish and told him that it was honey and goat's milk butter. He decided to give it a try and instantly fell in love with the rich honey taste.

By the time the main course was set in front of them, he was pretty sure anything the two of them cooked would be better than the most expensive meal he'd ever enjoyed.

The brisket was so juicy, it melted in his mouth.

Even the garlic mashed potatoes were beyond anything he could have imagined.

"You two should go into the restaurant business," Willow said when her plate was empty. "I can't remember the last time I had anything so wonderful."

"Thank you," both Charity and Ralph said at the same time.

"Wait until you taste Charity's apple pie." Ralph got up and took some of the empty plates with him. When he returned, he carried a pie plate and a carton of homemade ice cream.

Over dessert, Caleb finally broke his silence and talked about the plan that he and Ralph had come up with.

"We thought about giving him bad information, like we discussed, but taking it to a different level."

"How so?" Willow asked.

Chapter Thirteen

"Are you crazy?" Willow felt her heart jump as she slowly stood up, her fists on the table. She was breathing heavy, since she still couldn't believe the idea Caleb and Ralph had just laid out.

Caleb just looked at her, instead of answering.

"You plan on using yourself as bait?" When he nodded in agreement, she jumped in. "No!" She sat back down and took a couple deep breaths to steady herself. When she felt more under control, she took another bite of her mother's apple pie.

"No?" Caleb said, setting his fork down. "Just

no?"

"Yes." She tilted her head and felt like stomping her foot. "No."

"Well, I don't really see how it's up to you," he said, taking the last bite of his pie.

She chuckled. "I don't think it is, but I'm not letting you go through with it. Besides, it's a stupid plan."

"Oh, I suppose you have a better one?" Caleb glanced over when both her mother and Ralph quickly stood up and cleared the table.

"We'll just…" her mother said, nodding towards the kitchen.

"No need to rush off," Willow said calmly. "The discussion is over."

"No, it's not," Caleb grumbled and then stood up. "Thank you so much for the wonderful meal." He took her arm and pulled her gently until she was following him out of the house.

"Don't you see; this is the only way I can make sure you're safe." He turned on her once they'd stepped out onto the front porch.

"No it's not. It's a stupid plan that will only get you killed." She crossed her arms over her chest, determined to stay her ground.

"It's my decision." He started walking towards the cabin.

"No, it's not; it is ours. You don't get to put

yourself in danger and claim it's for me. Not without me being behind the plan." She rushed to keep up with him. The path was full of small pebbles, and the tall heels had caused her issues walking on the way over there, but he'd offered her his arm and they had made their way slowly. Now, she was almost jogging to keep up with him.

"My mind is already made up," he said, not slowing down. "Besides, it's better than just misleading them one more time." He stopped and turned towards her, causing her to bump solidly into his chest. His arms came up to steady her. "What's the point? If we just mislead them, it will only take a few more days or weeks for them to find us again. Do you really want to spend your entire life on the run like I have?"

That stopped her. He'd told her everything he'd gone through in the last thirteen years, but she'd never really put herself into his shoes. How it must have felt moving around so much. Always afraid to trust anyone or having to pick up and drop friendships at the drop of a hat.

"Trust me, Willa, this is the only way to make it end, once and for all."

"I don't like it." Her words came out as a whisper and she shivered in the night air, even though it was nearing eighty degrees out.

He pulled her closer and placed a kiss on her forehead. She felt warmth spreading from him to herself as she moved closer.

"You don't have to like it. It just has to work," he said into her hair.

"When do you plan on leaving?" She pulled back and looked into his dark eyes.

"Tomorrow."

She shook her head. "No, give it a few days. I'd like to see if we can come up with…"

"Willa, there's no other way."

"Please, just a few days," she begged.

His hands moved up and down her sides, and she felt his arousal pushed up against her. Instantly, desire rushed through every pore of her body, demanding she act quickly.

Pushing him with her hands, she shoved until his shoulders were up against the back of the barn. Her mouth fused with his as her fingers searched to free him.

"Promise me," she demanded.

"Willa," he said in a hoarse voice as finally she wrapped her fingers around his length. "My god," he whispered, just before he traded positions with her. Now, her back was up against the cool wood of the barn as his hands skated up her skirt. When he ripped the tiny triangle of silk covering her, she cried out, only to have his mouth cover the sound of pleasure. His fingers dipped into her, causing her hips to jump and follow his movements.

"Please," she begged, reaching for him. "Now."

"Willa," he gasped as her fingers dug into his hips, pulling him to her, guiding him where she wanted him.

When he thrust, she couldn't stop the desire from slamming through her, hard and fast. She'd wanted him just like this, his hands holding her up until she wrapped her legs around him as he thrust deeper into her.

His mouth was locked with hers, making her needs grow stronger. She'd never imagined she could feel so free and so tortured at the same time.

The solid wood walls behind her supported her as he continued his torment. She thought she heard him growl next to her ear, but she was too locked in experiencing her own pleasures to hear his exact words.

As she finally came back down to reality, she felt Caleb's breath against her neck, then the chill in the night air against her bare skin. It was then that she realized that Caleb was holding himself very stiff next to her. His breath was still falling over her exposed skin, but he wasn't moving except for the rise and fall of his chest.

"I've never said that to anyone before." It was almost a whisper next to her skin.

She tensed. Putting her hands on either side of his face, she forced him back so she could look at him.

"Why me? Why now?" she asked as a tear slid

down her cheek.

He closed his eyes and rested his forehead on hers. "I've never felt this way for anyone before." He pulled away, helping her adjust her skirt, then took her hand and started walking towards the cabin in silence.

When they walked in the door, he dropped her hand and walked over to the fireplace. He stood with his back to her and she could see the tension in his stance.

"Caleb." She walked towards him and started to open her mouth to say more, even though she wasn't sure what she was going to say, only that there was so much she wanted to tell him. But, before she could, her cell phone rang.

She rushed over to the counter, where she'd left it and saw her sister's photo and number. Taking a couple relaxing breaths, she answered.

"Hi." She tried to sound casual, but the fact that her heart was beating fast, thinking about Caleb and what he'd told her, didn't help the situation.

"How dare you." Wendy sounded mad. Mad, mad. "How could you tell my soon-to-be-husband to lie to me."

Willow sat down on the barstool and placed her head in her hands. "It wasn't—"

"No, you don't get to explain right now. Where are you?"

Willow thought about lying, but the truth was, if

Caleb was determined to go through with his plan, then telling her sister where she was wouldn't hurt.

"My mother's place."

"Good, stay put. We're coming for you."

"No!" She stood up and a moment later, Caleb's hands rested on her shoulders.

"Let them come," he said and she realized he'd been standing right behind her, listening in.

She pulled the phone from her ear and frowned at him. "No, I won't let you do this alone."

"Willa, I was never going to let you come along. Don't you see? It's my fault they found you in the first place. I have to end this. Alone."

She wanted to fight with him, but she could hear her sister trying to get her attention.

"Don't bother arguing, we're already in the car. We'll be there in less than half an hour." Her sister hung up and Willow started vibrating with anger. Slamming her phone done, she turned towards Caleb, ready to give him her full attitude.

Instead, he pulled her closer and just held on to her, killing all of the anger she'd been ready to release.

When he finally pulled back, tears were streaming down her face. "I've never felt this way about anyone else in my life either."

When he only nodded, she felt like he didn't

believe her. She wanted to say more.

"You'd better go change and get your things together." He was rubbing her arms and she noticed that she was chilled.

"I don't want to go with them. I want to stay here, with you."

He leaned down and placed a kiss on her lips. "Go." The simple word caused her to move her feet. She rushed up the stairs and felt like throwing herself down on the bed, but instead walked calmly into the bathroom and changed into her own jeans and shirt.

When she looked at herself in the mirror, she realized that her hair was a tangled mess and her makeup was running down her face from the tears she'd been silently crying.

She knew she had to come up with a different plan to help Caleb. One where she was sure he wouldn't spend the rest of his life running or end up dead. Maybe her sister would be able to help her out.

By the time she walked back downstairs, she felt a little more under control. Caleb was sitting at the bar, looking down at her phone, and she instantly had the most dreadful feeling rush over her.

"It's done," he said without turning towards Willow. He couldn't bear to see the hurt or fear in her eyes right now.

"What is?" He felt her move up behind him.

"I've talked to Agent Minster."

"Why? Why would you go through with this when I asked for more time?"

"I never agreed." He closed his eyes against the pain. "Besides, a few days isn't going to change the fact that sooner or later, they were going to find me."

"Us." She took his shoulders and turned him towards her. "I thought we were in this together?"

"Not anymore. Not after tomorrow."

"Do you have a death wish?" She took a step back. "Why would you do this?" Her voice had raised and the betrayal in her eyes was heartbreaking.

"No." He stood up and pulled her closer. "Trust me, I want nothing more than to find some cozy home and raise kids with you." He wrapped his arms around her, even though she tried to pull away. "I want to know what it feels like to experience my child kicking inside of you. To see how beautiful you look, holding him in your arms for the first time." He tugged her until her head rested on his shoulder. "To hear you sing him to sleep and to watch him grow." He felt tears stinging the backs of his eyes, so he swallowed all his dreams and pushed

175

away from her. "But none of that will be possible unless I do this one thing." He turned away and was thankful when he heard a knock at the door. "That must be your sister." He walked towards the front door.

When he opened the door, Wendy stood on the other side by her fiancé, Cole. He'd seen Cole Grayton on magazines and billboards. He'd even watched one of his surfing competitions. The guy was a great surfer, one of the best. But, in Caleb's life, surfing couldn't save you from a biker gang hell-bent on revenge.

"You must be…" He started to say, but Wendy reached out and before he could step back, she slapped him across the face. The loud crack echoed in the entryway.

"How dare you." Her voice vibrated as Cole held her arms to keep her from striking at him again. "I don't know who you think you are, storming into my sister's life and putting her in danger, but…"

"Wendy!" Willow rushed up behind him, taking his arm and pulling him back, away from her sister a step. "What the hell…"

"No, it's okay," he said, feeling the sting of the slap on his face. The slight pain helped wake him up to the situation at hand. "I'll leave you all to discuss—"

"No!" Willow took his hand in hers and stopped him from moving. "You're not going anywhere. Wendy, you owe Caleb an apology. He's done nothing but protect me since the moment…"

"The moment I came to you and put you in danger. She's right." He took her shoulders into his hands and turned her towards him. "It's fine. I have to leave anyway or I'll be late." He stopped himself from leaning down and placing a kiss on her lips, since he doubted her sister would allow it.

He stepped around the other couple and nodded a thanks to Cole for keeping his hold on Wendy. Then he made his way towards the main house, where he'd made arrangements to borrow Ralph's truck so he could complete his mission.

He was thankful she had her sister, mother, and Ralph. At least he knew they would do anything to keep her safe until this was all over.

His plan was a risky one, but if everything worked out, he might just still be alive by the end of tomorrow to enjoy a life with the only person he'd ever loved.

Chapter Fourteen

Willow watched Caleb walk away and felt like rushing after him and hitting him herself.

"Are you okay?" Her sister broke free of Cole's hold and rushed over to her, taking her into her arms.

"I'm fine. Really." She hugged Wendy back. "You're wrong about Caleb. He's the only reason I'm safe."

"From what you said, it sounds like he's the reason you're in danger in the first place."

Sure, it was true, but if he hadn't shown up at her apartment, he'd be dead. And, no matter what happened to her now, she couldn't imagine her life without him in it anymore.

He'd given her his heart and told her in the

sweetest words she'd ever heard, and she'd held back. Not out of fear of saying them, but out of fear of feeling them. She'd believed she'd loved before. Jake had been her high school sweetheart and her very first intimate experience. But after he'd gone off and joined the army, leaving her behind as he found and married his wife, she'd sworn off ever feeling that way about a man again.

Even her father had taught her how to hold back her feelings. She'd never really known if he was going to stick around for long. Isn't that what Caleb was making her feel now? She knew that if he could, he'd stay, but that kind of life just wasn't possible.

Not without her help. Looking at her sister and Cole, a new plan popped into her head. She thought about running after Caleb, but knew he'd try and talk her out of it. If her new plan was going to be successful, and if she hoped to save the man she had grown to love, she needed to do it all behind his back.

But first, she needed more details about his plan and where he was heading. And she knew exactly who to ask.

"Get your things. We're going to stay over at the Grayton's until this is all over." Her sister took her arm and started to walk her farther into the cabin.

Willow took a step away, still upset that her sister had such a closed mind about everything. "No. Don't you get it? This will never be over for him and it's all our father's fault. We owe it to Caleb to help him set his life right. He's spent his entire life running and for the first time, he has a chance to make it all stop."

"You don't get to bring Dad into this," her sister warned. "He died thirteen years ago after choosing this kind of dangerous life over his own daughters. He wasn't there for us when we needed him. He was never there for us!" her sister screamed as tears rolled down her face.

Willow took Wendy's shoulders, pulling her close. She hated to see her sister so upset, especially after all she'd done for her. She knew her next words would sting, but they needed to be said.

"But he was there for Caleb. He saved him. Gave him something he'd never experienced before. And then, because of it, he ruined the rest of his life. You're right, Dad wasn't there for us, but that doesn't mean we can turn our backs on someone who needs our help. The person who raised me"— she used her finger to wipe away a tear from her sister's face— "she taught me to be kind and generous. We need to do this now for Caleb, not only because he needs our help, but because of something that happened over thirteen years ago, which made him part of our family of sorts. And one thing my big sister taught me was you never turn your back on family."

Just then, there was a knock on the door. Cole opened it to her mother and Ralph. They both looked worried and Willow could see how uncomfortable her mother was to see Wendy standing in the entryway.

"Caleb just left. The meeting is set for early tomorrow morning at the pier," Ralph said as he put his arm around Charity's shoulders. Willow could tell he was trying to ease some of the tension everyone could see building in her.

Wendy stood back, her arms crossed over her chest. All the disdain her sister felt for their father had been nothing compared to what she felt for Willow's mother. Even though she'd tried a few years back to get her to reconcile with the woman, Wendy still disliked Charity.

"I need your help," Willow said to the room. "All of you. If we're going to help make sure Caleb is safe, really safe..." She looked around to the faces and knew asking for their help was the only way.

"First, we need to understand what this is all about. I don't understand why there are people after us. Who is Caleb?" Wendy still had her arms crossed over her chest.

"Maybe we should sit?" Willow said, nodding towards the sofas in the living room.

As soon as they sat down on the oversized sofas, her sister leaned forward and said, "Spill."

"How much did you know about Dad?" When her sister rolled her eyes, she cut in. "Summarize and humor me."

Wendy tilted her head. "Okay, I'll play this game." She leaned back as Cole wrapped an arm around her shoulders. "Dad, William Harvey Blake, born of Martha and John Blake in Jacksonville, Florida on May second. I can't remember the year."

Willow's mother broke in with the year, causing Wendy to frown in her direction.

"Dad never told me the same date twice. His parents died shortly after I was born, so I never got to know them. Nor my mother's, which was his first wife, Barbara. You know she died…"

"Yes," Willow broke in. "Continue about Dad."

Wendy's eyes closed for a moment, and then she continued. "Shortly after, he married your mother…" Her eyes moved to Charity once more.

"Yes, pass all that," Willow broke in, causing Wendy's eyebrows to shoot up. "His job," she supplied.

Wendy frowned. "As far as I know, he did odd jobs here and there when he was on the road. I'd always assumed he was a handyman of sorts."

Willow turned to her mother, who just nodded. "I had always assumed the same. He never really talked about that part of his life, especially the gang. I only knew the name, Lone Outlaws, never anything more."

"When did he first start riding bikes?" Willow asked.

"He was already riding when I met him," her mother answered, and a smile fell across her lips. "Actually, it was one of the main reasons I was attracted to him. My parents didn't like the bad-boy persona he had. Which, naturally, made me even more attracted to him."

Willow looked over to her sister who just shrugged. "I'm not sure. I have a picture of him sitting on a bike with me in his lap. I was in diapers."

"What about friends. Did he ever bring anyone around?" Willow looked between her sister and her mother.

Charity shook her head and Wendy shook hers more slowly. "Not that I can remember. What's this all about?" She leaned forward.

"Okay..." Willow proceeded to tell them all about what had happened weeks ago when Caleb showed up on her doorstep. Well, most of it anyway. She kept out the part about letting Caleb into her bed and into her heart.

When she was finally done with telling the story, her sister's face had turned a bright red and Willow knew that Wendy was about to explode.

"Why has it taken you this long to finally tell us all this?" Wendy crossed her arms over her chest as she asked in a low voice. Willow knew that any minute, her sister would start yelling.

"Because I was afraid you'd react like you're about to." She crossed her arms over her chest, much like the move her sister had made, and prepared herself.

Wendy, however, closed her eyes and took a few cleansing breaths.

"Do you have the journal with you?" Ralph asked.

She pulled it from the bottom of her purse, where she'd practically forgotten about it, and handed it over. She finished asking her sister questions as he flipped through the pages. When she was done, everyone sat in silence for a while.

Then Ralph turned to the back page of the journal and gasped.

"What?" everyone asked at the same time.

"Do you know what you have here?" He slowly stood up, his eyes still on the last page of the journal.

"No," Willow said, standing up as well. "What?"

"This is a key," he said.

"What?" She shook her head, not understanding, her eyes moving over to the journal. "How could a journal be a key?"

"Not a key, key." He twisted his wrist like he was unlocking a door. "But a *key*." He drew the word out. "These are file names." He flipped through the journal pages, pointing to all the letters and numbers. "And, this…"—he turned the journal around and pointed at her father's favorite saying—

185

"is the key."

"I don't understand." She reached out and took the book from him.

"Think computer files. Encrypted files. Ones that need a key or a phrase, such as this, to unlock."

Realization hit Willow quickly. "Who has the encrypted files?"

Ralph reached out and touched her lightly on the shoulder. "That, Willow, is exactly what we need to find out if we plan on saving Caleb."

The drive wasn't that long, but it was too quiet in the car as he traveled down the dark roads. He thought about everything that had happened to him over the last few weeks.

About how he'd met Willow, the first time he'd seen her standing on the beach, the wind taking her hair, the sun on her face. Then his mind flashed to the night in her apartment. When she'd leaned over him and patched him up. The first time he'd kissed her. He could still feel her lips on his. Her skin next to his. How wonderful she'd felt.

If, in the next few hours, he died, he would know that at least for one brief moment in his miserable life, he'd gotten to see what it felt like to hold onto heaven.

He knew his plan wasn't foolproof. Hell, when Ralph had offered him a gun, he'd thought hard about taking him up on it. But he knew the moment he stepped out of the car, it would be stripped from him. So, no matter what he did, he was walking into the fires of hell, pretty much naked.

He stopped the truck a block from the meeting place and waited and thought some more about Willow. When he could finally see the orange and red rays from the sun rising in the east, he glanced down at his watch. There was less than fifteen minutes before his life may be over. But, if all went well, Willow and Wendy would be safe for the rest of their lives.

Getting out of the truck, he grabbed his leather jacket and pulled it on. He tucked the truck keys in the pocket and started walking in the direction of the boardwalk.

For the first time in his life, he had something worth fighting for.

When he turned the corner, he could see a man in a dark suit standing near the end of the large abandoned pier. The chains to the wharf had been cut. Taking a deep breath, he started walking towards him slowly. The man watched as he approached.

"Minster." He stopped behind him.

"Caleb." The man's smiled spread as he looked at him.

"Thanks for meeting me on such short notice." Caleb felt a shiver run down his spine, but held perfectly still as he looked at the other man.

"I was curious about our little phone call. You said you had something new for me?"

"Yes, some more names and details," he lied as he leaned against the pier's railing, trying to look relaxed. "Why meet here?" Caleb asked. Looking around, he could just make out the almost empty beach. The parking lot had been completely vacant except for a dark black sedan, which he assumed was the agent's. There were a few people running along the shoreline, but even the little shop at the beginning of the pier hadn't opened its doors yet.

"I figured it would be easier on you. Now, what's this information you have?" Minster asked.

"Well..." Caleb went into his planned speech about the gang and all the information he'd known about from all those years ago. He could tell Minster was getting inpatient, but the man stood back and listened to the small details Caleb added into his story.

Finally, Caleb could see the man's patience leave.

"All this is old information. What's the new intel you hinted about?"

Just then, however, he was shocked to hear a voice behind him. He was sure his heart stopped beating for an entire minute.

"There you are," Willow said, rushing up the dock and right over to him. She leaned up on her toes to place a kiss on his lips. "I was beginning to think I wouldn't make it." She glanced over to the man standing beside him. "You must be Caleb's handler." She held out a hand and waited for him to shake hers, which he didn't.

"I'm sorry." The agent frowned at her. "I... I didn't know..."

"Oh, that's right. Caleb has been pretty tight lipped about me. I'm Willow Blake. William Blake was my father."

"What?" Caleb noticed the complete shock in the man's face before he quickly recovered. "I wasn't aware that Mr. Blake had a daughter."

Willow smiled and tucked her arm into Caleb's, squeezing it tightly. He thought he felt her shiver with fear, but he was still in so much shock, he wasn't sure of anything at this point.

"Two of us, actually. I was just going over some of my father's old things and stumbled on this old journal." She shocked Caleb further by pulling out the one thing that could have protected her and Wendy and handing it directly over to the man he suspected might be working for the bad guys.

"Willa—" She cut him off quickly, keeping her eyes locked with the agent.

"I was hoping maybe you could help me make heads or tails out of the darn thing." She tugged on his arm again and he was desperately trying to figure out what she was doing there.

"Yes, well." The agent's eyes scanned every page of the journal. "I'll be happy to take a look at—"

"Oh, how wonderful," Willow interrupted. "Now, I understand you are going to help Caleb and I move to a more secure location?"

The agent's eyes moved up to lock with Caleb's as he tucked her father's journal into his jacket pocket.

"Yes, well... You see, there's been a slight change of plans." When the man's hand pulled slowly out of the pocket, Caleb pushed Willow behind him as a sleek silver gun barrel pointed directly at his chest. "You see; I've made a few deals myself. I have someone else who's interested in *handling* you from this point on."

He felt Willow tense and shoved her farther behind him.

"Whoa." He held up his free hand. "I don't..." He tried to play dumb but tensed as he heard two other men walked up the abandoned pier behind them. They had been hiding behind a fishing shed area a few feet down the dock.

One of them grabbed Willow's arm and yanked her a few feet from him. When he reached to grab for her, the agent's arm swung out and hit him on the side of his head with the butt of his gun.

190

Caleb fell to his knees as stars exploded behind his eyes. He reached up and felt blood drip down his forehead. He stayed on his hands and knees, since he doubted the man was going to allow him to stand again anytime soon.

"Why are you doing this?" Willow cried out as she tried to fight the man who was holding her. "We trusted you." She glared over at Agent Minster.

The man chuckled and tucked his gun back into his jacket pocket, making a point to position it so it was still pointed in Caleb's direction. Caleb knew he'd use it if he had to. His eyes moved around, but the pier was still completely abandoned.

"I guess if you'd had your old man's information, you would have seen my name on his damn list and would have known I have been on the Lone Outlaws payroll for a long time."

"Why?" Willow cried out when Tony twisted her arm after her question.

"Enough. Time to go," Tony barked out.

"My father's journal." She tried to fight him. "You're in it?" Tony stopped when the agent signaled him to wait.

"Me and a few others were afraid that the contents of your father's journal would be found or that he'd come forward with our names. We'd heard about the journal when he'd first approached the agency with information against the gang. But after it was clear that your father hadn't come forward with all of the information, we stayed low, in hopes that it had been lost. Then, word got out that the journal was still floating around somewhere. [EE1] I naturally alerted the guys. I mean, he and your father are the reason they spent so much time locked up. We were watching Caleb, in hopes that he'd lead us back to Billy, but he never did."

"My father is dead. He died thirteen years ago," Willow blurted out.

"That explains why he never came back to the agency with the other information he'd promised after his initial reports." He laughed and leaned back against the railing. "Funny thing is, after he'd turned against and helped lock up most of the gang, it became stronger, more profitable. Sure, Ralphie was no longer in charge, and a few of the main guys were behind bars, but it turns out that wasn't such a bad thing after all. Was it Tony?"

Tony chuckled as he kept his eyes locked with Caleb's. "You could say being behind bars opened other doorways for us."

"You've been working with them the entire time? I trusted you," he growled.

"You should be careful who you trust," Minster said. "Yes, there's a lot of money to be made in and outside of the prison system, if you have the right connections. That's one of the main reasons we've employed a few more agents since your father's time. You'd be surprised how many guys want to make a few extra dollars on the side." The agent laughed and Caleb felt his anger grow.

Chapter Fifteen

*W*illow was trying to remain calm. She was afraid that the man holding her arms behind her back would discover the hidden wires and the recording device shoved into the back of her pants.

She tried to keep her eyes on Agent Minster. He was a tall, thin man in a very expensive looking suit. His jet-black hair was long and the high winds out on the end of the pier were blowing his hair directly into his eyes. He kept reaching up and swiping it aside, as if he was annoyed.

She knew she needed to get more information from the man before the team of heavily armed men would burst out of nowhere and save them both, but she was running out of ideas on how to get Agent Minster to talk without tipping him off.

She'd seen the anger in Caleb's eyes when he'd watched her walk towards him. She'd held him back from turning and walking away from the situation when she'd grabbed his arm.

"What's in the journal?" Caleb asked from his position on his knees.

She could see a trail of blood running down his left eyebrow where the agent had hit him with his gun.

Agent Minster chuckled as he started to walk back down the dock, without answering.

"If we're going to die because of it, we deserve to know." He fought off the other man, the one with the black eyepatch over one of his eyes, who had yanked him to his feet.

"Very well." The man glanced around and leaned back against the railing, looking quite comfortable, but highly out of place in a suit along the beach. "It's a trail."

"Of?" Caleb asked as he tried to yank his arm free from the other man.

"Bank accounts, which would lead the FBI directly to everyone who's ever benefited from the Lone Outlaws."

Caleb whistled. "That's a mighty long list," he

said, swiping the blood away from his eyes.

Agent Minster smiled, showing off his overly perfect white teeth. "You have no idea how far and wide our arms reach." He reached out, stretching his arms to his side as if to make a point. "County and state departments, government agencies, even foreign consulates and dignitaries. You name it!" The agent's voice rose a little before he straightened his jacket and brushed his dark hair back away from his eyes once more. "This"—he pulled out the journal— "is just the tip of the iceberg. We have major plans in the works. It's time we motivated this country into a better place. No more bending with the wind. Now is our time to make a stand." He glanced down and started flipping through the pages. Then his eyes moved over to hers when he reached the last page. "There's a page missing." He took a step towards her, showing her clearly where the last page had been torn out.

"It was never there," she lied, but he walked over and yanked her arm out from the other man's hold.

"Where is it?" he demanded.

"There was never a last page," she tried again, only to have her arm shoved high behind her back.

She called out in pain, only to be released a second later as Caleb's body slammed hard into them. They fell backwards onto the railing of the pier, which instantly gave way to the weight of three grown people.

Willow felt herself falling and reached out to

hold onto something, anything, as she fell fast. Something solid connected with her temple and she started to lose consciousness, only to be jolted awake again once she hit the water very hard.

She fought to surface from the deep water, kicking hard as she began to feel every place she'd impacted the water. Her left shoulder and wrist were on fire with the stinging pain.

When she broke the surface, she gasped air into her lungs and glanced around. Caleb still had a hold on the agent. His arms were locked around the man's neck as he kept trying to reach for what Willow could only assume was the gun in his jacket. She started to swim towards them, thinking she would be able to help Caleb, but then watched in horror as the two men slid below the surface of the deep water, still fighting.

She looked up just in time to watch one of the other two men jump into the water and land only a few feet away from her. Her head and wrist was throbbing, but she kicked off and started to make her way towards the shore. The water pushed her under the pier. A wave pushed her farther out, slamming her knee into a large wooden support beam. Pain shot up her leg as she tried to kick herself free from the current. Finally, she was back in open water, but then she was yanked and pulled under the water by very large hands.

She kicked out, salt water rushing into her mouth as she tried to scream. Her fingernails scraped down the man's arms as she tried to free the hold he had on her hair as he held her head under.

Then the man was yanked away and she was free from his hold as she was pushed up onto a surfboard. Her lungs felt like they were on fire as she gulped in air. Her eyes watered as she blinked and looked up into Cole's smiling face.

"Thought you might need some help," he joked as he held the unconscious man's head up, next to them in the water.

"Caleb?" she asked, her throat scratchy from swallowing water.

"My brothers have him." He nodded his wet blond head towards the left. When she looked, Caleb was sitting on a much larger surfboard with Marcus. Agent Minster was lying face down on another long board as Roman paddled towards them.

Cole kicked off, paddling really fast towards the shore. There were over two dozen agents in full SWAT gear waiting for them along the shoreline. They were the first ones to reach the beach.

The agents helped her off the smaller surfboard and wrapped a large blanket around her shoulders. When they tried to walk her up towards their waiting trucks, she pushed them away and watched, waiting for Caleb to rush out of the water towards her.

His arms wrapped around her, lifting her as he held her close. She felt herself start to shake as tears rolled down her face.

"I thought…" She cried out.

"What were you thinking?" He pulled back, his hands going to her shoulders. "I could have lost you."

She blinked a few times and shook her head. "I could say the same about you." She tried to cross her arms over her chest, only to cry out when her wrist turned.

"You're hurt?" His fingers took her arm, holding her still. "She's hurt," he called out, only to have several people flock around her.

For the next half an hour, she wasn't alone with Caleb again. She rode in the back of an ambulance to the local hospital a few miles away. By the time her arm was x-rayed, her clothes were completely dry. Caleb silently sat across from her in the tiny room, waiting for the doctor to let her know if her wrist was broken, as nurses came and went.

"What were you thinking?" he asked again. This time there was less anger in his tone.

"I was thinking of you." She leaned back, her eyes going to his.

"You could have gotten yourself killed."

"So could you. Why did you go alone?"

"I didn't," he said, walking over to her and taking her good hand into his own.

"What?"

"Remember my plan to call the agency?"

She nodded. "But when I called them, they knew nothing about your plans. That's why I thought…"

"What? That I'd lied? That I had a death wish?"

She nodded, feeling tears slide down her face.

"Willow, I don't know who you talked to, but at least half of the agents on the beach where there because of me."

"I called the CIA. Who did you call?"

"The FBI." He chuckled. "Sounds like they'll be fighting it out over who gets to deal with the gang." He pulled her hand up and placed a kiss on her knuckles. "Why the CIA? They shouldn't have anything to do with this."

"They do, actually. It seems there's a lot of national security information in my father's files."

"Files?" He sat next to her.

She nodded. "His journal. All of it was file names with the key to unlock them all being, *Places to go, people to meet*." He shook his head. "It's complicated. But apparently my new stepfather understands it all much better than I do." She chuckled.

"Speaking of which…" they heard from the door. Looking over, they saw her mother and Ralph standing just outside the curtain.

"How did it go?" Her mother rushed over to her, taking her into a light hug.

"Not as smooth as we'd hoped." She held up her wrapped wrist.

"It's not broken," Caleb assured her, shaking Ralph's hand.

"It better not be," Wendy said as she rushed into the room. "Had I known it was going to be this dangerous... I would have never..."

Cole walked up behind her and took her shoulders and turned her back out the door. "Sorry, we'll just go sit out in the waiting room." He nodded to a nurse, who was about to tell them there were too many people in the small area.

Willow chuckled. "I'll see you in a while," she called out.

"You'd better..." she heard Wendy call back.

When she looked over, she saw Caleb smiling.

"I do believe I like her," he said.

"Even though she slapped you?"

His smile fell away. "I deserved it."

"We'll just head out ourselves," Ralph said, taking her mother's hand and walking out of the room.

"You didn't do anything wrong. Besides, if you hadn't come to me, where would you be now?"

201

"Dead."

She nodded. "Exactly." She brought his hand up to her lips. "And I can't bear the thought of not having known you."

He leaned down until his forehead rested on hers. "My god. What am I going to do with you?"

"Marry me. I hope." Her eyes focused on his as he pulled back.

"It's not possible," he said after a moment of silence.

"Why? Because you don't love me?"

He shook his head no.

"Because you're married to someone else?"

Once more he shook his head no, a slight smile on his lips.

"You don't believe in marriage?"

Again, he shook his head, a full smile now on his lips.

"Then I see no reason we can't get married.

He sighed and she watched the heaviness of his life begin to lift behind his eyes.

"Caleb, if I've proven one thing to you today, it's that I'll follow you no matter where you go or what danger you're in." She reached up and took his face in her hands. "I want to be with you for the rest of my life. As you said, I want to have children with you, watch them grow—" His lips crushed down on hers, stopping her next words.

His fingers shook as he brushed a strand of hair from her face. His lips heated hers, forcing her entire body to melt against his as he wrapped his arms around her shoulders.

"Fine, I'll marry you," he said and she could hear the laughter in his voice. "On one condition."

"Anything." She smiled up at him.

"We buy a new sofa," he joked.

She laughed and nodded in agreement.

Chapter Sixteen

Caleb stood on the soft sand and waited along with the other people. The wait seemed to last forever since the sun was almost blinding him. The light jacket he was wearing seemed to absorb his sweat. Must be the rich material, he thought. He'd never owned anything as nice as what he was currently wearing. Now he had a closet full of clothes like it. Not to mention the new car he drove every day to and from his job. A job he was very grateful for having.

It seemed it paid to have a family, of sorts. The Graytons had not only welcomed him in, but had quickly given him a job as construction manager at

Paradise Construction, one of Marcus and Roman's businesses.

He not only loved the work but loved having a steady income. The added bonus of knowing he wouldn't have to pack up and move only made things better.

Now, living with Willow in her tiny apartment, he was looking forward to having a normal life, something he'd never imagined he could ever have.

One of the first things they had done as a couple was go furniture shopping. The new cream-colored leather sofa was the first piece of furniture he'd ever bought with his own money.

Even Wendy was starting to like him. She'd warmed up to Charity and Ralph coming around more often as well. He could tell that Willow still struggled with trusting her mother but knew she was trying hard every time they got together with them.

It had taken a few weeks to finally clear things up with both the FBI and the CIA. Actually, he'd been shocked when one of the agencies had offered him a job. But since he was done living on the edge and running, he'd easily turned them down.

Now, with all of Willow's father's files decrypted, they knew exactly who had been behind everything and who to target. Apparently, the gang's influence had reached far and wide, spreading even into some of the top terrorist groups that had grown in power over the last twenty years.

Thanks to Billy's journal, more than a hundred people were awaiting trial or in custody, with many more names being placed on international watch lists.

Major terrorist activity had been tied to some of the names on the list, and millions of dollars of funds could be traced back to the list, as well.

Some of the top people on the list had amassed a lot of power over the last thirteen years. Several had seats in top government positions. It was the biggest scandal since Watergate. Or so all the news stations had reported.

But thanks to the promise from both agencies, their names were kept tightly sealed in the files. He was feeling more secure than he'd ever felt in his entire life on the run. Maybe it had been his meeting with the commander in chief himself, along with his promise that anyone who came after him would guard his secrets.

Just then, he noticed that the music had changed and everyone turned and stood to watch the progression. He stood with everyone else and smiles when his eyes zeroed in on his prize. She looked even more beautiful than he remembered.

Her long hair blew in the soft breeze floating off the warm waters as the sun sunk lower in the sky. Just seeing her smile caused his knees to go weak. He was sure everyone in the small crowd could see the way he looked at her, but he didn't care. For now, she was his.

It seemed there had been a few more surprises than he'd bargained for when he'd decided to stick around Surf Breeze. His eyes went to Willow's belly under the flowing skirt of her bridesmaid dress.

They hadn't told anyone yet, since Willow didn't want to take away from her sister's big day, but in less than seven months, they were going to welcome the son or daughter he'd never imagined he could ever have.

He was sure his smile and the silly look he had in his eyes would give his secret away. Especially since every time he touched her, his hands cupped her small belly.

Willow had been determined not to push their wedding date up, and was planning on a date sometime early next spring. She wanted their baby to take part in their happy day, so they could come together as a family.

He, for his part, was happy giving her exactly what she wanted, as long as it was for the rest of his life.

Willow's steps almost faltered when her eyes connected with Caleb's. She wasn't sure, since the sun was setting behind him, but she thought she saw tears in those dark eyes of his.

She held the small bouquet of flowers over her belly, in hopes that it would help settle the nausea that she'd felt the last few hours. She could tell that Wendy had known something was up, and as she was pulling on her bridesmaid dress, her sister had walked into the room, rushed over to her, and hugged her.

Still, Willow hadn't said anything, but when Wendy pulled back, she could see acknowledgement in her sister's eyes.

"When?" she'd asked.

"Early March," she'd whispered.

Her sister's smile grew bigger. "Remind me to slap that man of yours again for keeping this from us."

Willow had chuckled. "On that note, he reminded me to tell you that you could use a few boxing lessons."

"Tell him I'd be happy to take him on any day." Her sister had hugged her again.

She couldn't wait to tell Caleb how Wendy had reacted to their news. Nor could she wait until they moved into Wendy's bigger condo in a few weeks. Of course, her sister knew nothing about moving yet, since Cole was surprising her with a house as a wedding gift. But Willow and Caleb had made arrangements with Cole to move into her sister's two-bedroom condo along the beach once he finally sprang the gift on her.

She stopped now at the end of the small aisle and turned with her back to the setting sun. The entire Grayton clan stood in the first two rows. Cassey and Luke held hands as she leaned from one foot to the other, shifting her very large belly. Marcus and Shelly held their small bundle, their daughter, Rose. Roman and Missy stood on either side of their son Reagan, who looked bored and kept his eyes on the water, no doubt wishing, he could strip off his suit and jump in.

Willow turned her head towards her soon-to-be brother-in-law, who was standing next to her by a small archway made out of coral shells. The man looked like he was ready to jump out of his skin. It was funny; Willow had never seen Cole dressed in anything other than swim shorts and T-shirts. Seeing him now, dressed in an off-white cotton suit, she realized just how truly handsome he was.

Her eyes moved back towards Caleb. There was only one man that made her heart jump and he was looking directly at her as if she did the same thing to him. She smiled at him until her sister walked up the aisle between the chairs.

The cool evening breeze blew her long blonde hair away from her face. Willow and Wendy had matching flower wreaths in their hair, but Wendy's was twice the size and had a larger mixture of colorful flowers, which were tied up in her locks.

Her sister's wedding dress hung off her tan

shoulders and hugged her slender build until just above her knees, where it flowered out and was caught in the soft breeze. She'd never seen her sister look happier or more beautiful.

Wendy stopped a foot away from Cole, and their eyes locked as they reached out and took one another's hands. Willow stood by and listened to her sister give her vows to the man she loved, but her eyes kept creeping back to the man she loved.

Tears stung her eyes when Cole leaned in and kissed her sister as everyone erupted into cheers. Then, before she knew it, Caleb was by her side, his arms around her as he tugged her towards the water.

"What are you…?" she asked, laughing as he pulled her right to the edge of the water. She glanced over as everyone at the wedding was laughing and congratulating her sister and Cole.

"We never really made this official," he said, pulling a small box from his jacket pocket. When he got down on one knee right there in front of everyone, she felt her heart skip. Her hands moved over her heart and she held her breath.

"Caleb, you didn't…" She didn't get any further, before Marcus yelled out.

"It's about time!"

Someone else shouted. "Get it over with."

Caleb laughed up at her from his position in the sand. Water rushed up, soaking his pant legs, but he didn't seem to notice.

"Willow, I've never had a family. I never had parents to teach me right from wrong, but one thing you've shown me is that we are right together. I want to spend the rest of my life making you smile and laugh. Seeing your blue eyes go soft when I touch you." He opened the box and held it towards her. "Will you marry me?"

She smiled down at him. "You've shown me so much in the last few months. I'm the luckiest woman alive to have you as my family. Of course I'll marry you." She no more than got those words out, than she was being lifted and spun around as his lips brushed over hers.

They heard the cheers and yells from the wedding party a few feet away. When she gripped his shoulders and warned him that she might lose her lunch if he didn't stop spinning, he laughed and set her back on her feet.

Then he reached down and took her hand in his and started walking back towards their family. She would have never imagined that she'd have such a wonderful group of people care so much for her. Glancing over, she realized that no matter what happened from here on out, that they were now the part of the best family in the world.

The End

Sneak peek - Finding Pride

Chapter One

As the sun disappeared behind a dark cloud, a white sedan crept slowly down the winding road. A wall of trees on either side gave the impression that the only way out was to forge ahead. The black pavement weaved around tight bends, up and down rolling hills. If you could witness the scene from above, it would appear similar to a white mouse running through a maze on its way to find some cheese.

Several minutes had passed since the last open field. Every now and then a quick glance of a farmhouse or a barn would appear. But for now, the only view was the gray of the sky, the green of the trees, and the dark surface of the road.

The car was traveling towards freedom that had come at the worst price: death. Megan Kimble had just lost the last of her family.

Hours later, the sun peeked out of the clouds, landing on the small crowd gathered around a casket. Mist and fog hung in the afternoon air. The sun's rays made the hill overlooking the small town of Pride, Oregon, appear to be cut off from civilization, like an island floating in a sea of fog. Not a sound came from the gathered mourners.

Each person stood with their head down, looking at the dark, wet wood of the casket.

Megan stood in front of the crowd dressed in a dark skirt and a black raincoat. She looked down as tears silently rolled down her cheeks. Her long blonde hair was neatly tied back with a clip. The right sleeve of her coat hung empty, and her arm was tucked close to her body, encased in a white cast from her upper arm to just above her wrist.

Looking up, she gazed around the cemetery, not really noticing the people, only the old and crumbled headstones. Her eyes paused on a tall figure in the distance that appeared to hover above the mist. Blinking a few times to clear the moisture from her eyes, she realized it was a huge headstone in the shape of an angel with arms outstretched towards the heavens. It seemed to be reaching up in desperation, in need of a helping hand to ascend above.

Her thoughts drifted to Matt, and she looked back down at the casket. He had always called her his little angel. Looking at the simple wooden casket through teary eyes, she remembered her brother's face as it looked fifteen years ago when she had awakened in a hospital bed with her young body covered in bruises, the memories of violence by her father's hand gone, along with their parents' lives.

Matt's was the first face she had seen in the cold sterile room. His face had been streaked with tears, his eyes red as he'd comforted her. "Little Meg,

216

everything will be okay. I'll take care of you now. Don't worry my little angel."

Her thoughts snapped back to the cemetery as they lowered the casket into the wet ground. What had she ever done to deserve such a great brother? What had she ever given back to him? He'd given up everything for her, yet she couldn't think of one thing she'd given him except lies.

Feeling hopeless and isolated, she began to wonder what she had left to live for. Why continue? She was all alone now; there was no one left to share her life with. Realizing it was probably Derek's influence causing her dark thoughts, she tensed. Lifting her head, she tried to dismiss the thoughts of her ex-husband. He didn't matter anymore, she told herself. He was out of her life forever.

As she stood in the old cemetery surrounded by a hundred strangers, she felt utterly alone. Matt had been her family, the only family that had really mattered. She had an aunt somewhere, but she hadn't seen or heard from the woman in over fifteen years.

Glancing over, she noticed the priest walking towards her and quickly wiped the tears from her face. He was a short, stout man who was dressed in long, black robes. He wore a wide-brimmed hat that covered his curly silver hair. His face seemed gentle and kind. She could see that his eyes were red from his own tears. He had been very generous in the words he'd spoken about her brother during the short service.

She wasn't Catholic. Neither was her brother, but at this point she wasn't going to object. It had been a wonderful service and so many people had turned out. She didn't know who had organized the service, but she was sure that the priest had had a big hand in it.

"Hello, dear, I'm Father Michael. We spoke on the phone a few days ago," he said, as he took her by the hand. His hands were warm and comforting. "Matt was such a nice young man. I'll miss him dearly."

"Thank you. I'm sorry I wasn't able to get here sooner. I would have helped you plan his service-"

"Don't mention it. We all pitched in to help. That's the wonderful thing about small towns." He smiled and patted her hand a little. "The people in Pride don't usually take to strangers, but Matt just fit in. He became part of the family, you might say. I know he wasn't Catholic, but he did enjoy a good sermon and always attended our social events. Your brother was very well liked around here."

It didn't sound like he was talking about her brother. Matt had always been somewhat of a loner and had never really taken to crowds. But then again, they'd grown apart from each other when he'd moved out west to Oregon.

As the priest continued talking to her about Matt and the town of Pride, she looked around at the crowd of strangers in the muddy cemetery. It appeared that the whole town had braved the wet weather for her brother's funeral. There were numerous faces, both young and old, many weatherworn from years on local fishing boats. She was used to being in crowds, having lived in a large city most of her life, but now it felt like every set of eyes were on her.

Shaking her head clear and taking another look around, she could see that, in fact, almost no one was looking directly at her. As her eyes scanned around, something else caught her gaze. A pair of the lightest silver-blue eyes she'd ever seen looked back at her through the crowd. The man stood a head taller than everyone else around him, and he was staring directly at her. For a moment, she forgot everything, including blinking.

The man had dark brown wavy hair, which was a little long and reached over his coat collar. From what she could see of him under his leather coat, he appeared to be thin. His face could have easily been etched in marble and put on display. His jaw was strong with the smallest of clefts in his chin. His lips were full and his nose was straight, but it was his eyes that caught her attention again. He was staring at her like he wanted to say something to her from across the crowded cemetery.

When Father Michael stepped between them, he broke the trance she'd been in. Blinking, she tried to refocus on the short priest. He was attempting to encourage her to stop by the church for services sometime.

"Megan, I feel like you're already part of the flock. I'm sure we'll be seeing you next week. If there is anything we can do for you, just let me know," the father said while patting her hand. "You will let us know if you need any help moving in, what with your hurt arm and all."

She looked down at her right arm enclosed in the white cast. She had it tucked closely under her raincoat, which she had left unzipped. The pain was a dull throb now, but that didn't make the terrible memories go away.

"The Jordan's are your nearest neighbors. They were very good friends of Matt's. The two boys are young and strong. I'm sure they'll be glad to come down and help you move in your things." There was a matchmaking look in the man's eyes, and she tried to take a step backwards, but her hand was still engulfed by his larger one. "And I'm sure their sister is looking forward to getting them out of her hair for a few hours," he said with a wink.

"Thank you, Father. I'll try to stop by the church for services. I don't have much to move in, only a few bags, but thank you for offering." It was the truth. Megan had sold what little furniture she had left. In fact, she'd been living out of her suitcase for the past few weeks.

"Well, now, if you change your mind, let me know," he said, patting her hand one more time.

Just then a large woman walked up to them. She had on a very bright blue dress covered in white flowers. Over it, she had a slick black raincoat that covered only half of the dress and half of the woman. She reminded Megan of a peacock all dressed up with its feathers ruffled.

"Father Michael, you let go of that girl's hand so I can shake it. It's a great pleasure to finally meet you, Megan," the woman said while shaking her hand with a firm, warm grip. "I'm Patty O'Neil. I run the local grocery store. I've heard lots about you from your dear departed brother, God bless him." The woman quickly crossed herself and continued. "I'm sure proud to finally meet you. O'Neil's Grocery. It's right down on Main Street. You can't miss it," she said. "It's been in my family for generations. Well, if there is anything we can do…" She trailed off as the next person approached her.

And so it went, the entire town shaking her hand and offering their help in any manner possible.

Todd Jordan silently watched Matt's younger sister. He'd recognized her instantly from the picture Matt had kept on his desk. She was a lot thinner now and very pale. She looked lost. Her broken arm, which she held against her tiny body, made her look even more so. He'd scanned her from head to toe when she'd arrived at the cemetery. The raincoat she wore reached halfway down her slender body, and her heels looked very sensible as they sat halfway sunk in the mud.

He remembered Matt telling him that she was recently divorced but couldn't remember any more details. All he knew was that his friend hadn't been happy about the circumstances. His thoughts were interrupted when Father Michael approached him.

"Well, now, young Todd." The father always called him "young" even though he was now in his mid-thirties. "It's a shame, yes, sir. Her heart is broken. It is your duty as Matt's best friend to make sure you and your family help her settle in. Such a lovely thing, too. To think she'll be living in that old, drafty house all by herself." The father shook his head.

Matt's house wasn't drafty. If anything, it was in better shape than his own. He could tell the good father was probably up to his old matchmaking schemes.

"And to think, the poor girl will be moving in all by herself, and in the state she's in, too. She could hardly shake my hand." Here it comes, he thought, as his gaze once again swept over to where the object of their conversation stood. She was now surrounded by half the town and looked very lost.

"You need to do the right thing by Matt and make sure his little sister gets settled in safely. God has some answers for her. She's come halfway across the world all alone to bury her poor brother." Father Michael shook his head. "I want you to promise me that you and your family will stop by the house often, you hear me?" he said with a sad look on his face.

Todd's gaze swept back to the priest. He knew that look. It was the same look he and a friend had gotten in high school after sneaking in to the cemetery with the Blake girls to try to scare them on Halloween night. The father had tried to scold them, but the entire time, he had been laughing at them, instead.

"Yes, Father," he murmured. Father Michael nodded his head and turned away to greet another group of people.

Todd looked back over at Megan and saw that she was even paler than before. He grabbed his sister's arm as she was walking past him and nodded in Megan's direction.

"Someone needs to go save her," he said under his breath.

"What do you suggest I do?" Lacey said with a stern look, placing both hands on her small hips.

"I don't know. You're the one who's good at breaking things...up," he added after his sister's eyes heated. Then he grabbed her shoulders and pointed her in Megan's direction.

He saw Lacey's shoulders slump a little after taking in the sight of Megan being swamped by the whole of Pride.

"Humph," Lacey grunted and started marching towards the growing crowd. His sister may be small, but she packed the biggest punch in town.

Megan stood there as an older gentleman talked to her. She hadn't caught his name when he'd barged to the front of the line and grabbed her hand.

"I didn't know Matt all that well, but he was a nice young man. He always had wonderful things to say about my bar, never once starting a brawl. Broke a couple up, though," the bar owner said with a crooked grin. "Always such a nice m-m-m," he started to stutter.

Concerned, she quickly looked up from the man's hand, which was tightly gripping her own. Standing beside the bar owner was a pixie. Megan didn't believe in fairy tales, but there was no other way to describe the woman. Megan had a strong urge to walk around the petite creature and see if wings were tucked under her dark purple raincoat. The woman was perfect, from the tip of her pixie-cut black hair to the toes of her green galoshes. Galoshes, Megan noted, that didn't have a speck of dirt on them. She was shorter than Megan and very petite with rounder curves. Her skin was fair and her eyes were a crystal gray blue. She had a cute nose that turned up slightly at the end and full lips that were a light shade of pink. She also had a commanding look on her face.

The bar owner literally backed away without

even finishing his sentence, then he quickly walked away without so much as a glance back. Within seconds, everyone who'd gathered around her had wandered off, all without a single word from the pixie.

"How...?" Megan's voice squeaked, so she cleared her throat and started again, "How did you do that?"

"Well, it takes years of practice," the pixie said with a smile. "I'm Lacey Jordan." Her voice was smoky and laced with sexuality. "I was very good friends with your brother. I'm sorry he's gone."

The simple words touched something inside Megan. She could tell there was truth behind them. Lacey reached over and lightly grabbed Megan's good arm and then led her towards a row of parked cars.

"I'm also your neighbor. Shall we get you in out of the weather and home where you belong? We've made some meat pie for dinner, and I'm sure by the time we get there, the whole town will be right behind us. We'll go get my brothers and take you home."

"Oh, please, I don't want to be a bother. I'll be fine." Megan felt compelled to follow the small woman who still had a light hold on her arm and an air of command that surrounded her.

"Nonsense! It's no bother at all. Plus, if you turn down dinner," she said with a slight smile, "my brother Iian might get his feelings hurt. It's not every day he makes the family's famous dish." She continued walking towards the row of cars. "Come on then, let's get you out of this rain."

Megan looked up at the skies and at that exact moment, it started to lightly rain. Her mouth fell open in shock, but when a big fat drop landed on her bottom lip, she quickly closed it. Lacey was still lightly holding her arm and pulling her towards the parked cars near the side of the small white church.

Having not eaten before her flight to Portland, Megan felt her stomach growl. Exhaustion was settling in, and she felt a chill come over her bones. She wasn't sure what meat pie was, but if it had meat in it, she knew she could tolerate it.

"Oh! I'm sorry." She stopped walking, and Lacey turned and looked at her. "I forgot to mention that I have a rental car over there." She pointed slightly with her injured arm towards a small white sedan that she'd hastily rented at the airport four hours earlier.

"Give me the keys and my brothers can drive it over to the house for you," Lacey said, waving towards a man who had the same rich black hair. He'd been standing towards the back of the buildings in the shadows, so far back that Megan hadn't even noticed he was there.

As he stepped out, she saw that his hair was longer than his sister's. The man strolled over, appearing to be in no hurry, and he looked like he rather enjoyed the nasty weather and his surroundings. To say that he was tall would be an understatement; he must have been six and half feet and it only took him a couple of strides to reach where they stood.

Megan had to crane her neck to look up into his face, and she noticed that he had the same light eyes as his sister. His chin was strong with a tiny cleft, and his lips held a lazy smile that made him look rather harmless. Lacey handed him the keys to the rental car, then waved her hands in a sequence of patterns in front of her.

Lacey turned back to her. "Megan, this is my brother Iian. He's hearing impaired and uses sign language to communicate, but he can also read lips really well," she said while continuing to sign. Then turning her face away from his she said, "He likes to eavesdrop, so be careful what you say while facing him."

Smiling, Megan turned back to Iian in time to see the quick flash of humor in his eyes as he signed something to his sister. She gestured something back to him and hit him on the shoulder in a sisterly way.

"Come on, Megan. Iian will take care of your car." They began walking towards the cars as the rain came down harder. Groups of people without umbrellas were quickly sprinting to their vehicles. Others with umbrellas were making their way more slowly.

When Megan sank into the passenger seat of Lacey's sedan, chills ran up and down her spine. Lacey got in behind the wheel and started the engine. She turned the heater on full blast, and as it started to warm the inside of the car, Megan felt she could happily fall asleep right there.

They pulled away from the small church and the now-empty cemetery. The windshield wipers were clearing the rain from her view with a soft squeak, but Megan still felt like she wasn't able to see much beyond the path that the headlights were cutting through the fog. Then she sat up a little straighter and looked over at Lacey, who had her eyes on the road. Realizing she had just gotten into a stranger's car, she tensed. What did she really know about this small woman?

"You don't need to worry," Lacey said, not taking her eyes off the road. "I'm not going to kidnap you." She turned her head slightly and smiled. "We'll deliver you to your brother's house before everyone else gets there. I hope you don't mind, but we invited a few close friends over for potluck. It's what Matt would have wanted, something small. Your brother was very well liked around town, and people will want to bid him goodbye in this manner." She smiled sadly.

"Of course." She relaxed a little and rested her head against the window, enjoying the soft hum of the engine and the gentle beat of the wipers. By the time they pulled off the main road, the sky was dark; the sun hadn't come back out before setting for the night.

"Here we are now." Lacey parked the car so the headlights hit the house full force. "Matt spent most of the first year remodeling the place. I think you'll like what he's done with it." Lacey smiled at her.

Looking through the car window, Megan saw a large, white two-story house. Long green shutters sat on either side of picture windows that lined the whole front of the house. The front door was bright red with a brass knocker, and there were stained-glass windows on either side of the door. The windows seemed to glow brightly in the night.

Following Lacey's lead, she opened her door, and together they raced for the front porch through the light rain. Standing on the huge, brightly lit covered porch, she watched Lacey open the front door with a key from her own key chain. As they crossed the threshold, Megan's rental car pulled up in the driveway and parked next to Lacey's sedan.

Watching from the doorway, she saw Iian step out of the car along with the silver-blue-eyed man she had seen in the cemetery. Both men looked up to the front door and nodded to her and then stepped behind the rental car and started pulling her overnight bags from the trunk.

"They'll get those. Come on inside out of the cold," Lacey said. She walked towards the back of the house, leaving Megan standing alone in her brother's doorway.

Even though her brother had lived here for several years, she'd never visited Oregon before today. There had always been a reason not to visit him. Looking down at the cast on her arm, she realized that this was the reason she'd put off the last visit. The broken arm had been one more thing she had hidden from her brother, and she wished that she hadn't postponed that last trip.

Quickly turning into the house, she tried to avoid thinking about her brother and her regrets. Lacey was walking back towards her from the back of a long hallway, rubbing her hands together for warmth.

Just then, both men walked onto the front porch and shook their heads like dogs, shaking the rain from their hair. They wiped their feet on the wire mat before crossing into the entryway.

Megan noted that their faces were very similar, yet she could see subtle differences in the men. Their height and weight for one. Iian was slightly taller, with a broader build. And although the brothers shared the same gorgeous eyes, it was the depth of the one brother's that captured her attention again.

"Megan, this is my older brother, Todd," Lacey said from behind her.

Todd nodded his hello and looked at her, causing warmth to spread throughout her.

"It's chilly in here. Will you please start a fire in the living room before the guests arrive?" Lacey asked him.

Again, a nod was his only reply, and then he turned and went into the dark room to the right without saying a word.

"Iian," Lacey said and signed along, "please take those up to Matt's room and start a fire up there."

Lacey walked away, turning on lights as she went. Iian jogged up the curved staircase that sat to the left of the entryway. He had her suitcase in one arm like it weighed nothing and had thrown her overnight bag over his shoulder. It had taken all of her strength to drag those two bags through the airport that morning. His hair was still dripping wet and he was humming to himself. Humming? Megan thought.

As everyone bustled around, starting fires and turning on lights, Megan stood in the main entryway. She felt useless all over again. Here she was standing in her brother's home, letting strangers take care of her. Hadn't she promised herself that she would take care of herself from now on? But she was so tired. She didn't think that letting these people help her out for one night would hurt.

Lacey came back into the entryway. "Come on, let's get you out of that wet coat." Lacey reached for the rain jacket as Megan flinched away. Slowly Lacey's hands returned to her side.

"I'm sorry," Megan began, looking down at her

hands, not wanting to look Lacey in the eyes. "I'm just a bit jumpy and tired I suppose." She tried to smile. How could she explain she didn't like to be touched?

"No need to apologize," Lacey said, warmly. "You must be overwhelmed. I'm sure a bit hungry by now, too. At any rate, people will start arriving any minute, and I'm sure there will be lots of food." As Lacey finished those words, the doorbell rang. "Go on in and have a seat by the fire. I'll take care of this."

Lacey pointed Megan in the direction of the two French doors that Todd had disappeared through earlier. Slowly walking towards them, Megan listened as Lacey greeted a group of people. Not really wanting to deal with anyone yet, she slipped inside the softly lit room and sighed as she rested against the wall.

Todd was across the room, bent over a pile of wood in the fireplace, blowing on flames that had started on some crumpled papers. He'd removed his leather jacket, and she noticed that he was wearing a white dress shirt that was stretched taut over his muscular arms. Powerful, was the word that came to her mind. She was nervous around powerful, so instead of walking over to the warmth of the fire, she turned back towards the doorway and watched Lacey greet everyone.

She was about to walk out to the hall and try to find the kitchen, when she felt hands lightly placed on her shoulders. Out of reflex, she jumped and spun around, her hand raised in defense.

"Easy," Todd murmured. "Let me take your coat; you're soaking wet." He held his hands out as one would to a wounded animal.

Blushing, she said, "I'm sorry. You startled me." She hung her head and turned around so that he wouldn't see her face turning red. Her heart was racing and her hands started shaking. It still affected her, being touched.

Gently, he helped her out of her jacket, being extra careful around her right arm. He hung it next to his coat on an oak rack by the door. When he noticed Lacey watching from the doorway, he said to her, "She can eat by the fire. She's frozen."

Lacey nodded in agreement. "There's a TV tray over in the corner. Go on, I'll bring a plate of food in once it's heated."

Father Michael had just walked into the house and was standing in the doorway with a few other people. Todd nodded to them then quickly walked her back into the living room under several watchful eyes. His hand gently cupped her good elbow.

Megan followed him back towards the fireplace where the room was warmer. She held her hand out towards the fire. She hadn't realized how freezing she was until the warmth hit her, causing her hand to tingle.

"I'm sorry. I didn't realize how cold I was until now," she said nervously to the room. She knew

Todd was still behind her but didn't wanted to turn and look at him just yet. Closing her eyes, she let out the breath she'd been holding since he'd touched her. She was nervous around him, around men. When he touched her, however feather light it was, it was like a power surge rushing through her body. She'd been avoiding getting close to anyone for so long that she knew she was out of practice. Taking a deep breath, she turned to the quiet room.

"You have his eyes." He interrupted her thoughts. He stood right inside the doors, his hands buried deep in his pockets as he watched her.

Megan was about to say something, anything, but just then Iian came into the room with a smile on his face. He stopped and took one look at his brother and then at her and signed something quickly to Todd. She wasn't sure what he said, but Todd gave his brother a frustrated look and then walked out of the room without saying a word to either of them.

Iian walked over to her and took her hand in his and said in a rich, warm voice, "Megan, I am very sorry about Matt."

Gasping, she realized she wasn't aware he could speak.

He smiled slightly. "I can speak. I lost my hearing in an accident when I was eighteen. I don't do it very often; my brother and sister say I have the most annoying voice."

She could hear the little blunders he made with

234

his voice, as if he was out of practice. But he had such a rich, deep voice, so much like his brother's.

Speaking slowly and making sure to keep her face directed at his, she said, "You have a wonderful voice, rich and warm. Thank you for taking care of my luggage and starting a fire upstairs."

He smiled, while still holding her hand in his warm one. "You're chilled. Come over and sit down." He pulled her towards a dark-colored couch near the fireplace. "Lacey is still greeting people, but I'm sure you'll have a plate of food in front of you in no time. I'll sit with you and keep you company until then."

Back in the kitchen, Todd was helping his sister with the food, but his mind was back in the living room. He'd guessed by the look in Megan's eyes and the way she had jumped at his light touch that someone had hurt her, and recently too. The look on her face was heartbreaking, and he didn't care to see it on Matt's little sister. He was glad she'd turned away when she had, so she couldn't see the sadness and anger that had come into his eyes. Had Matt known this was going on? What she'd been going through? He didn't think so, but that didn't keep him from wanting to hunt someone down for the pain they had caused her.

His sister had seen the look on his face; she

always saw everything. She had shaken her head at him and discreetly signed to him not to look so serious, that he might scare her. He'd quickly dropped his eyes and hidden it. He'd been so concerned about her, he hadn't even realized that his face had shown it.

Earlier, he'd watched Megan when she'd gone to the fire. She had started to relax and had rolled her shoulders, showing him a hint of her long white neck. He'd felt a flash of desire so strong that he had winced. That was when Iian had entered the room and signed for him not to look so serious. Was he that serious of a person that both his siblings had to warn him about it in one day? He didn't want to scare Megan, but he couldn't control the way his emotions played out on his face.

His brother and sister had a way of seeing things for what they were, which always annoyed him. At this point, he couldn't even muster up enough strength to go in there and talk with his brother about his feelings. He knew he wouldn't get anywhere talking about it with Lacey, but he could at least hold his own with Iian.

Hearing people roam about the house, he could just imagine Iian and Megan in the other room talking. His brother had a way of making women feel very comfortable and at ease. Thinking about them getting together, he realized that maybe he did have enough strength to go talk to his brother about his feelings.

As he walked towards the kitchen door to go and

do just that, Lacey stopped him with one word. "Don't."

He turned to her ready to argue, but she only smiled at him.

Quickly, he let his breath out in a loud puff.

"How is it that you can defuse any situation with that smile?" he said, pulling her into a hug. "You drive me nuts."

She sighed and hugged him back, resting her head on his chest. "Give her time, Todd. Let Iian talk to her a while. She's going to need to trust us. She's had it hard." Taking a deep breath and a step back, she grabbed a plate of food and handed it to him. "Now, go take this to her, and no more strange looks!" She smiled as she pushed him out the door.

Every bone in his body said that his sister was right, but his blood was boiling so hot he wanted answers. Matt had been like a brother to him, not just his best friend. What hurt Matt, hurt him. He missed his friend and felt sad, angry, and lost about his death. He knew Matt would've wanted them to take care of Megan and so he was going to make sure she was taken care of, period.

He knew that his brother and sister felt the same way about her as he did. Megan was family now. But he couldn't deny the quick pull he'd felt when he looked into those sea green eyes of hers.

Other books by Jill Sanders

The Pride Series
Finding Pride
Discovering Pride
Returning Pride
Lasting Pride
Serving Pride
Red Hot Christmas
My Sweet Valentine
Return To Me
Rescue Me

The Secret Series
Secret Seduction
Secret Pleasure
Secret Guardian
Secret Passions
Secret Identity
Secret Sauce

The West Series
Loving Lauren
Taming Alex
Holding Haley
Missy's Moment
Breaking Travis
Roping Ryan
Wild Bride
Corey's Catch

The Grayton Series
Last Resort
Someday Beach
Rip Current
In Too Deep
Swept Away

Lucky Series
Unlucky In Love
Sweet Resolve

For a complete list of books, visit
http://jillsanders.com

PRINT ISBN:1519475799
DIGITAL ISBN: 978-1-942896-12-8
Copyright © 2015 Jill Sanders
Copyeditor: Erica Ellis – inkdeepediting.com

About the Author

Jill Sanders is *The New York Times* and *USA Today* bestselling author of the Pride, Secret, West, Grayton, and Lucky Series romance novels. She continues to lure new readers with her sweet and sexy stories. Her books are available in every English-speaking country as audiobooks and are now being translated into different languages.

Born as an identical twin to a large family, she was raised in the Pacific Northwest and later relocated to Colorado for college and a successful IT career before discovering her talent as a writer. She now makes her home along the Emerald Coast in Florida where she enjoys the beach, hiking, swimming, wine-tasting, and of course writing.

Connect with Jill on Facebook: http://fb.com/JillSandersBooks

Twitter: @JillMSanders or visit her Web site at http://JillSanders.com

4637

Made in the USA
Lexington, KY
06 January 2016